Porch Girls

Terry D. Bible

ROYSTON
Publishing

BK Royston Publishing
P. O. Box 4321
Jeffersonville, IN 47131
502-802-5385
http://www.bkroystonpublishing.com
bkroystonpublishing@gmail.com

Cover Design: Bill Lacy
Purchase Standard License for
Shutterstock.com Bill Meier image

ISBN-13:978-1-946111-04-3
ISBN-10:1-946111-04-X

Printed in the United States of America

Dedication

It is to my deepest gratitude and dedication to my favorite women in the Quinton Family.

GREAT- GRANDMOTHER
Maggie Patton Cannon

GRANDMOTHER
Hattie Mae Cannon Irvin Carter

MOTHER
Jacqueline Lorene Harding Bradley

Acknowledgement

I never would've had this book published had I not listened to my late mother Mrs. Jacqueline Lorene Harding Bradley.

To my dearest friend, Sandra Anderson Bouggess for giving me encouragement and the boldness to succeed in my endeavors. "Hail Central High!

I'm also truly grateful to my insurance agent, Mr. Louis Coleman for selling me a Toshiba 95 Windows Laptop in 2001.

Giving Praises to God for Rev. Gregory Smith of Hill Street Baptist Church for allowing me to have evening classes with him to learn about my computer in 2002.

Thanks to Mr. Tony Holley for being my "Computer Technician" helping me out in the late hours of the night.

Thanks to the Sally Bingham's Kentucky Foundation for Women's "The HopScotch House" for developing solitude and peace even when I was going through a "storm" in my life.

Ms. Shirley Hurley was so kind and patient with me as I browsed through a lot of books in the library and participated in meditation through faith that I will succeed with "Porch Girls".

Foremost and for all, to give thanks to my Lord and Savior Jesus Christ for giving me such fantastic insight and the women in my life as the "seeds of my life" to achieve my goals.

Terry D. Bible

Table of Contents

Character List

Elijah Poohtawn- Chief Cherokee

Susie Poohtawn Quinton- Matriarch, daughter of Elijah that marries Caucasian Quinton John- Big Papa- 1st generation

Hilda Poohtawn- Susie sister

Geneva Quinton- daughter of Susie- 2nd generation

Aunt Margaret- Geneva sister

Josephine Quinton- daughter of Geneva- 3rd generation

Tisha Mingo Quinton (Thomas) - 4th generation

Miss Lynn- Josephine best friend

Granddaddy Bernard- Geneva's husband

Felicia and Sukey

Jackie- Tisha's sister

Aunt Shayla- Geneva and Bernard's
daughter

Aunt Mary Catherine- Josie's long
lost sister

Cousin Dot- Josie's cousin- Aunt
Margaret daughter

Aunt Betty- Josie's wild sister

Albert- Josie's husband

Aunt Louise- Geneva & Margaret
baby sister

Aunt Thelma - Hilda's daughter, Susie
niece

The Essence of Porch Girls

I need to reiterate myself of what Porch Girls means:

Porch Girls in itself is a metaphor of strength, knowledge, pain, love, and humor. It is LIFE! The kind of life that will make you realize what is going to make you do, be, and know to make you get off that "porch" when your time comes to free yourself.

First, there is the "worldly" porch, the porch that you see people performing abominations unto the Lord such as shooting craps, having drugs, and alcohol in their possession to be seen early in the morning with their debris in the yard for the garbage men to pick up.

Second, there is the "quiet" porch, the porch that doesn't allow anyone to come sit to "fellowship" and yet will tell everything that's been going on the night before. Even when they go to church, they're the ones that's telling everybody's business on the street.

Third, there is the "free" porch, this is the porch that allows everybody and anybody on their porch to edify, identify, and modify what's going on in the neighborhood, the streets, and everywhere else in the community.

Consequently, you could "trust" these people for they will look out for you, but don't cross them. They could be your worst enemy.

Last but not least, there is the "screen" porch. The hidden porch that are so beautiful, as you sit on them with their high priced furniture with the gray iron legs, the glass stained table top and the chairs with the so-called silk and cotton pads to sit in the them. The porch will be covered with beautiful flowers that will have the evergreen bushes surrounding the area, so that no one can see what they're doing.

Consequently, they're the ones that will be doing EVERYTHING! In spite of these different "Porches", a lot of depth of despair, pain, hope, disillusion, joy and of course love came from these porches to convey the people to live their lives as they saw fit.

Frankly, I saw it as a way of life, but I saw it as a way of death. A death in a way because you couldn't breathe to go, except to the bathroom, you couldn't express yourself without any conviction, you couldn't explore your horizons without questions, and you couldn't expand your talent without decisions from yourself.

Because of these porches that I have mentioned, it did bring a lot of prominence, vigilance, and ignorance to the people in this world to gain, maintain, and sustain some understanding and wisdom to know the difference between good and evil.

And to those, I may add that had the patience to be obedient and subservient to God that survived in their endeavors. Hopefully this book will give you the endurance and stamina to overcome your fears to step off the "Porch" to "Stand" and be proud of yourself to be the man or woman you represent in your family emotionally, spiritually, educationally, mentally, and socially.

Explore your own world, to indulge yourself to read a book, music, engage in a hobby, or whatever else that can help you expand your mind from going on the wrong path of life. It's a terrible world out there. It brings me back to remember that old saying "If you can't hang with the big boys, STAY on the porch!"

Introduction

PORCH GIRLS--- A VINTAGE STORY

This is a story about four generations of black-American women struggling for freedom, justice, and respect in our so called America. Through four generations, the Quinton women were strong, vibrant, talented and beautiful. Like a female spider, they weaved their way through the mainstream of life to maintain their dignity to love their family and strived to make their goals prosperous and rewarding.

As we take the journey back into the 19th century of pure treachery and deceit, to go forward into the remarkable Age of Aquarius, the Quinton women tried to make their lives through music, history, and songs. Susie Quinton was the sole matriarch in the family. With her strong American Native background, Susie paved her way through the prejudice and racism of her hometown Okochee County, Florida to migrate to Louisville, Kentucky to raise her four children.

So it was in my great-grandmother's time, RACISM kept my Great-grandmother Susie on the porch. Until she violated the white man's rules to do what she wanted. Needless to say, how could it be imperative for Susie Quinton to marry a white man to make it better? So she thought. Instead they were ignored, slighted, but not indignant enough to be a Quinton in their social world. So the Quinton girls turned their resentfulness, pain, and disillusion into the streets for comfort.

It caused a lot of emotional scars to act out negatively in their lives. No pride, no dignity, no self-esteem, no courage, no peace ran through this family bloodline from then on.

Until Geneva, my grandmother, a dark distinguished woman with her Indian descent, her skin which shined liked the grease on a black iron skillet and her hair shiny like the moon in the winter's night.

An adventurous, aggressive, independent woman that wouldn't take nothing for her journey, strove to stay distant from her mothers' whims and tactics to keep her on the "porch." Adding on to the family tree was my mother Josephine Quinton. Josephine was a strong, driven, black, and intelligent woman that always had mouth almighty and tongue everlasting. Josie always gave her mother the last word, until that very last time my grandmother Geneva saw that her daughter leave her house.

So Josephine took an adverse turn in her life at an early age because she didn't finish school. Last but not least, then came Tisha Mingo Quinton. The fourth generation that was born with the fire of intensity, tenacious energy, and with an adventurous spirit like her Great-grandmother, with much purpose of strength like her mother. Justice and honesty are strongholds in Tisha's life in which she shows her family that she is going to struggle from the childhood antics, and the sexual persuasive-ness in her life. Tisha Mingo is going to win the struggle to get off the "porch" to gain the free spirit that she intends to let go and live her life.

Chapter 1
THE TRAIL OF TEARS

It was 1832 and the "Trail of Tears" had begun. The Cherokee Indians had to migrate to Oklahoma, which was a land that they knew nothing about. Through the storms, the rain from the Northwest whence they came, through the mountains and the valleys, thousands of Indians died trying to make the move. My great-great grandfather was one of them.

President Andrew Jackson was president at this time and had signed the Indian Removal Act in 1830. President Martin Van Buren expedited the process for Cherokee Indians to be moved to reservations in the West, which made matters worse. Migration was horrible and that one event deliberately changed the Cherokee's life forever.

Elijah Poohtawn was a Cherokee Chief after his father died. His father died in the Battle of

Chickamauga. My great-great grandfather Elijah had to hold up the banner to keep his people alive as they traveled to the Natchez Trace in Tennessee. As they stopped in Tennessee to rest, some of the tribe were discussing their decision to settle there rather than to go on to Florida.

"He will be on your back like a sneaky snake in the grass. Remember what my father taught you." Elijah said to his people.

It was in the evening, as the beautiful orange sun settled in the West, the Great White Spirit painted the sky with purple and orange clouds as if He was looking down on them.

Elijah was tired, but couldn't help hearing his people's mumbling. "Listen up! I know that some of you want to settle here. I'm not going to stop you. My Father told me to keep going to Florida where the Seminoles stay. By time the sun rises, if there are those that want to travel with me, come with me. For those that want to stay, stay. Remember to settle where there is water and plenty of vegetation. The white man watches you in this strange land, the spirit of our Fathers will be watching you."

Half of the tribe stayed in Williamson County in the state of Tennessee. The hills looked vibrant and strong. The valleys were low with beautiful meadows filled with a water stream that came from a strong river called the "Tennessee River." As the tribes gathered to leave, Elijah's cousin decided to stay. His cousin came to embrace Elijah.

In Indian language, Elijah said, "Peace be unto you." (It was like the story in the Bible in the book of Genesis 13' verse 8 that talks about Abraham and his nephew Lot.)

"Take care of yourself Lone Wolf. Take care of our people," Elijah's cousin said.

As they gave each other the Indian brace sign, Elijah started his way to Florida. The Indians started chanting their way to Florida. Elijah thought about staying, but his Father's dreams kept him from staying. The Cherokee were tired, but they loved Elijah's father, for he was a Great Leader. After fighting President William Harrison in the 1840's about the railroad, the Cheyenne tribe fought until the bitter end.

Elijah walked proudly. His coal black hair falling down his back as the sun made it look blue. His height giving him such a physique of a lion proudly walking through the strange terrain as he looked out for his people. He had his cousin, The Bear, to protect him, and he had the Eagle to look after him.

As the tribe approached Florida on the border of Alabama, Elijah's people began to fall ill. He stopped them and inquired, "I need somebody to go into town to get some goods."

There was a young Indian named Little Feather. He came up to Elijah and said, "I know a little white man's talk. I'll go and give it a try."

"The Great Spirit will bless you if you do this task," Elijah replied to Little Feather.

4

The Alabama border was serene and sufficient. The area gave the Indians a sense of peace and serenity for the moment so that they could get some rest. Elijah told the young Indian, "Go and get some Cod Liver Oil and some blankets if they have them. I'm going to send Running Bear with you. We need some milk for the children also. Don't be afraid. We won't be far. If the white man harasses you, tell them that you come from the border of Tennessee and you got lost or something. They won't come looking for anyone. After all, they hate us. The Great Spirit in the Sky is looking after you so that you will be able to bring us the goods."

As the two Indians went toward town, they came upon the General Store. Some white boys started to harass Little Feather. The white boys fought Little Feather while Running Bear went into the store to get the goods.

All of a sudden, a white woman screamed, "Indians!"

Running Bear and Little Feather ran up a ridge to get to the border in Florida. Elijah noticed that his people were getting sick in the new climate. He gathered the old, female Indians to place them in a tent with the children to get some sleep. The rest of the men went out into the woods to see what they could gather for medicine.

It was dark. The night sky brought the moon with great light, and Little Feather and Running Bear had not returned. Elijah was getting worried. He gathered scouts to look for them.

Within a moment, they heard some voices in Indian language to tell them that some white men were behind them. Elijah quickly hid the women and children in a ravine, while the men hid in the oak trees to see what was happening. About ten white men were chasing Running Bear and Little Feather. The Indians began shooting arrows from the thick trees as the white men were shooting at them.

The Indians had killed about five of the white men with their bow and arrows. Once the white men were realized that their men were dead, they turned around to go back, for they couldn't see in the dark like the Indians could. Elijah had to grab Little Feather by his feet to keep him from falling off the ridge. Running Bear was right near them, appearing as Elijah ran with Little Feather.

They were one hundred feet from the rest of the tribe. The Indians came down from the trees. Little Feather was gasping for breath to tell Elijah what happened as he went into town.

Little Feather caught his breath and said, "I went into town. As I approached the General Store, these young white boys started fighting me. I tried to ignore them but they just kept fighting me. As I was fighting the boys, Running Bear sneaked into the store, and a white woman hollered, "Indians!" By that time, Running Bear had picked up all the goods that he could. I ran off while some white men came running to shoot at us. As they were shooting at us, we ran up to the mountain. That's when you grabbed me, Great Elijah, by my feet, as I was about to fall in the deep ravine."

By this time, both Little Feather was still trying to catch his breath. Running Bear was catching his breath.

Elijah asked Running Bear. "Well, did you get anything?"

Running Bear pulled out five blankets. Running Bear had some tonic that was supposed to stop coughing. The Indians didn't have the right herbs to help them to get healed, so they took what the white man had, and their horses, too.

Elijah grabbed Running Bear with a bear hug. They laughed out loud with pride and dignity. Little Feather looked so proud to have Elijah and Running Bear to hug him too.

Elijah realized that someone was coming and said, "We've got to move out shortly. The white men are going to come very early. Let's see if we can make a canvas on which to put the elderly women. Let the younger women with child be put upon the horses and put the blankets on them."

Meanwhile, the white men came returned quickly on their horses to town. As they hurried off their horses to go into the saloon, they saw that the patrons were drunk. Some women were sitting on the laps of some of the men when the Sheriff shot a gun into the air.

"Everybody listen up! The Deputy hollered out. "Some Indians came into town today to steal some goods out of the General Store. We need to get them."

Everybody in the saloon hollered out in agreement.

"Let's get them in the morning," someone yelled.

"Yeah! Cause I shore ain't going to get them tonight," someone else said while looking hungrily at the women.

Everybody started laughing except for one white man, who stood in the corner of the saloon, looking at all of them.

He got up from his chair and the Sheriff stopped him and asked, "You going somewhere, stranger?"

The white man answered, "I don't have to answer to you. I'm going to my room. That is, if that's all right with you."

The Sheriff got out of the stranger's way and watched him walk into the hotel. The stranger hurried to his room to get his belongings so he could go find the Indians and warn them about what was coming. The stranger kept his hotel light on and situated pillows to appear like a person in the window to throw the Sheriff off. However, the Sheriff got distracted by one of the saloon women. The stranger was able to leave out of the back of the hotel and swiftly ride his horse away.

At that time, Elijah and his people were moving fast through the woods. Elijah heard a horse behind them, but he didn't want to alarm the others. He trailed back on his feet to see who it was. It was the stranger. Elijah hooked the stranger with a limb to throw him off his horse and down to the ground. "Who are you?" Elijah asked, with his red eyes shining in the dark like a wolf.

The stranger looked scared but was bold enough to speak. "My name is Vance Edmond, and I want to help you."

"I don't need your help," Elijah said angrily.

"Yes, you do." Vance said. "You are heading toward a mountain. If you would turn east to get off the mountain, you will head toward another river to get you to Florida."

"How do you know that's where I'm headed?" Elijah asked.

Vance answered, "Because that's where I'm heading. The white men are coming after you. By morning, you and your people will be already hitting Florida. They won't be able to get you then."

Elijah asked Vance. "Why are you helping me?"

Vance looked at Elijah, "I've been following you since Tennessee. To be frank with you, my ancestors have been with Indians as far as the Alamo. I won't go into my family history, but I will tell you this, I've never like the white man's ways. I will help an Indian before I will help them. I'm not a renegade from the War. I'll tell you that I'm half-Indian myself. Let's just leave it at that."

It was getting into dawn. Fifty Indians followed Elijah as they were coming upon a river to get to Florida. Thank the Great Spirit in the Sky, for there was a bridge to cross; the Indians were getting excited to see the beautiful river to cross the land they have been waiting to see. Vance stuck with them. Running Bear was half sleep when he noticed that a white man was with the tribe. Running Bear ran up to Elijah to tell him that the people needed to rest.

As Running Bear stares at Vance, Elijah reassures Running Bear that everything is all right. The sun was rising in the East as the white men caught up with the Indians. The Indians were able to cut the strong rope that supported the bridge. Running Bear was reassured when he saw what the stranger had done for them.

All three of them looked at the white men behind them and laughed together as they continued to travel on their way. As the evening approached, the moon was coming up and shining like a glow of white crystal that beamed on the earth to see clearly on the cool ground. Elijah had his people to stop to get some rest under some weeping willow trees with long branches that reached to the ground as if they were crying. The Indians thought they were beautiful.

As the wind was blowing in their faces, the children laid down to sleep; the older ones were feeling their problems were going away. The older men killed about thirty rabbits for the women to skin and cook for the next day.

There wasn't a white man in sight. When the children got up the next morning, they played in the ravine. The women were gathering dinner, for everyone was waiting for the feast. The men were discussing which way to travel the next day, because tomorrow would be here before they knew it. Vance was resting by a strong oak tree.

As Vance watched the Indians celebrating and enjoying themselves, he spotted a beautiful Indian woman that had a body shaped like an hourglass. Her beautiful black hair glowed in the moonlight. The Indian woman was looking at Vance, too.

While the Indian woman stared at Vance's eyes, she saw that he was half-Indian. Elijah, Running Bear, and Little Feather all noticed what was going on. The Indian woman walked toward Vance. She said, "I'm Running Deer. Why don't you tell my people who you really are?" Vance was alarmed as he turned around to see that Elijah was looking dead at him as he looked at the woman.

"I told your Leader who I am. I didn't think that I had to answer to a beautiful woman, too."

The Indian woman smiled. "Thank you for the compliment. You still haven't answered my question."

Vance looked at the woman for a moment, and then started to walk away. The Indian woman walked in front of him. "Did I say something wrong?"

At that moment, Vance was gazing at the woman as if she was his wife a long time ago.

Vance was a widower; his wife was murdered by white men somewhere back in Kansas. She was killed because the white men didn't like him coming into town. When the white men saw that he stopped to get some goods, they began to harass his wife as she waited for her husband in the buggy. She screamed and Vance came out of the store to fight the men.

When he jumped on one of the men, the people in the town just watched the action, but didn't intervene. One of the white men pulled his gun to shoot Vance, but shot Vance's wife instead. Vance held his wife as the life left her body. This was the memory he was thinking of as he gazed at the Indian woman in front of him. "I had a wife that looked just like you."

"So sorry to hear that," she replied.

"It's alright. Once I help your Leader get to his destination, I'm taking a different route east of Florida," Vance said.

"It's getting late. Don't you think that you should be getting some sleep?" she asked.

The Indian woman looked at him with a frustrated expression, because he was missing her obvious proposition. She grabbed Vance by his head to give him a wet kiss that made him grab her hungrily in return, for he hadn't had any loving for a very long time. Vance gently laid her down on the ground to make love to her. He missed those days when he was with his wife.

They stopped kissing each other. Vance rubbed her breasts where her nipples were sticking up hard, waiting to be sucked. Vance grabbed her breast gently with his mouth. Running Deer raised up her dress so that Vance could receive what she had to offer. Vance took the offer, and as they climaxed together a wolf in the woods howled loudly. Running Deer yelled, and Vance took a deep breath holding her, as if he didn't want to separate from her body. She looked at him with so much gratitude; she kissed Vance and then got up, leaving him on the ground.

It was dawn. The sky was a peaceful blue. Vance was startled awake by a rabbit as it brushed by him; he got up and kindled a fire. The Indians started to reappear from their hiding places. Vance remembered what he had done the night before. He saw some Indians come to escort him to Elijah.

Vance knew what was going to happen. (When you couple with an Indian woman in a tribe, the man is obligated to take her for a wife).

As Vance went into Elijah's tent, Elijah wore a serious look on his face. "You have traveled a long way with us. You know that it's time for you to go."

"Yes, I know," Vance answered. "Tallahassee is not far from here. The best that I can do is to make sure that there is no more danger to you. As we travel on our way, I want to thank you for allowing me to be with your people."

Elijah asked Vance, "Was your wife Indian too?" Vance knew then that Elijah knew about him and Running Deer. Vance looked surprised as he stood silently.

Elijah told Vance, "You can have Running Deer. She wants to be with you anyway." Vance didn't know what to say. "Go!" said Elijah. "May the Great Spirit in the Sky bless you and Running Deer for many moons."

The Indians were happy. They started to pack as the Indians began to excitedly beat on their drums. Their hearts were beating with the beat of the drums, to receive the spirit of the Great Father in the sky.

It was early summer, as the evening came upon them, Vance went to Elijah to tell him that he was taking another route. Tallahassee was fifty miles from them. Vance Edmond and Running Deer took their horses to go east. Running Bear watched as he waved farewell to the both of them.

As they gave each other the Indian handshake, the Indians moved fast. Elijah chose four men to scout around the area to see if they could be in any danger. The Indians walked toward Tallahassee. It was beautiful with palm trees and willows, and the ground was so moist that the Indians would have no problem growing their crops.

Elijah pointed to the destination on which stood a fort that was once held in the 1800s when

President Andrew Jackson massacred a lot of blacks and Indians. He was supposed to meet some Indian settlers there. The settlers were looking their best as they walked proudly to greet the other Indians.

Proud Eagle came to greet Elijah. "Welcome, Elijah. I know that you must be tired from your long journey. Come! I will show you where you can settle in. There is a lot to tell you about this land. You must know the white men have been giving us a lot of trouble. They want us to move farther inland to where the swamps are. Here they have a Council for Indian Affairs."

Elijah asked, "When do we meet, because I'm not going to take anything else from the white man. I'm tired. You know that my cousin Lone Wolf stayed in Tennessee." Proud Eagle looked distraught as he took Elijah into his small dwelling.

Proud Eagle had all kinds of dead animals on the wall. Over the fireplace, there was an

Indian blanket that represented the Cheyenne tribe that had many eagle feathers surrounding the blanket, which had brown, black, and white colors woven throughout the blanket. As Elijah slumped in a big, brown leather chair, an Indian woman came to serve Elijah some herbal tea.

Proud Eagle told Elijah that everything was all right with the current situation. Proud Eagle told Elijah that he heard about white men in Tennessee forcing Lone Wolf to settle on some dry land away from the great waters. Elijah shook his head and said, "I told Lone Eagle to not leave me. You can't tell these young people anything."

By that time as they were finishing their drinks, some of the Indian men came in to tell the two great leaders that it was time for the celebration to start. "Here, you can dress in my guest room. I will go prepare for the celebration." Proud Eagle smiled and embraced Elijah as he left his house. "I'm so happy that you are here."

The Indians were ready to celebrate; they began to exchange gifts and find good spots to enjoy the festivities. The Indians who were performing started to dance and beat on the drums. They moved around and shook their percussions instruments all around the people. They started to chant and sing their welcome song.

As they stopped dancing and chanting, Elijah walked out into the circle for Proud Eagle to come to hand Elijah a scepter. Elijah takes it and bowed to Proud Eagle. He walked away deliberately. As Elijah walked to his seat beside Proud Eagle, everybody stood up to shout. The drums continued to beat all evening. Elijah took a deep breath in awe. He made it to the new land that his father Snow Cloud told him about. Proud Eagle had been in Florida way before the Battle of The Little Big Horn.

He knew how nasty President William Lloyd Harrison was during the Battle of Chickamauga, and he knew that there were some black Indians called the "Buffalo Soldiers." Proud Eagle traveled south with a hundred Indians. The Buffalo Soldiers helped him get there. Elijah watched the Indian women scattered around the land with their babies, but Elijah had his eyes on one particular Indian woman. Proud Eagle interrupted Elijah's thoughts. "In the morning, we will take a walk around. There are some prospects that I wanted to show you. Then I will show you where the Council is being held."

Elijah attempted to excuse himself from Proud Eagle's company, saying that he was tired after eating such a good feast from the celebration. Proud Eagle took the hint. "Yes, I understand, Elijah. I have lots of women here. They are good women. I see that you have your eyes set on Snow Feather." Proud Eagle was smiling proudly. "Well, you'll have plenty of time to choose the one you want."

Elijah rose from the chair to say, "Yes, of course. I'm going to turn in. I can hardly see straight." Elijah said good night and walked toward the house where Proud Eagle stayed until Snow Feather came walking towards him. "Did you enjoy yourself Great One?"

Elijah turned around to see Snow Feather. His tight eyes squinted to stare at Snow Feather. He pretended that he did not know she was there. "Oh! Excuse me. I didn't see you there."

"I just wanted to say welcome." Snow Feather smiled and walked away. Elijah stared at the woman, for he didn't notice that she was propositioning him. Morning came quick while the village was quiet and serene. Elijah awoke and noticed that the Indian women had breakfast already prepared for him. He slumped back into the bed to contemplate about last night.

Seeing Snow Feather right in front of him, he dreams of holding her in his arms, kissing her and making love to her. All of a sudden, the door knocks to open to see Snow Feather dressed in a beautiful white gown, her large breasts exposed from her bodice. Elijah rises from the bed to greet her and takes her by the hand to guide her to his bed. He lays her gently down and kisses her passionately.

Snow Feather's black hair hung long and wavy down on her back. Elijah moves her hair from her face as he pulls her gown off her smooth, olive shoulders and begins to kiss her breast like a hungry man. Snow Feather opened her legs to greet Elijah as she held him tight to her breast. It seemed that Elijah couldn't get enough of Snow Feather's love. When they climaxed together, they kissed each other so softly and slow that Elijah stopped to look in Snow Feather's dark eyes to see that love was under a new light.

A gracious light he needed to see, for he had been lonely for quite some time. Snow Feather smiled at Elijah. Elijah pulls to him and says. "I want you to be my woman."

Snow Feather answered. "I've so wanted to hear those words from you." Elijah followed Snow Feather to the window to see the beautiful blue sky. It was clear like glass.

The sun shone brightly the next morning. It filled the room with such light that Elijah couldn't help but to stop kissing Snow Feather. Elijah asked her, "Will I see you this evening? I am going to some places with Proud Eagle." Proud Eagle was about to enter the guest room when he saw them together. Snow Feather leaves Elijah as she kissed him on his chest.

Elijah watched Snow Feather leave the room. He nods his head to go into the bathroom to get dressed for the day. Proud Eagle knocked on the door. "Can I come in?"

Elijah turned and said, "Come in." Elijah pulled his hair back and put a feather in it. Proud Eagle looked at the rumpled condition of Elijah's bed and asked, "Well, are you ready for the big day?" His eyebrows went up and he chuckled. Elijah looked surprise and embarrassed, but his grin was a mile wide.

Elijah answered by grabbing his cloak. Proud Eagle and Elijah struck out to walk around the beautiful terrain that the Indians had settled in. As the mountains from side to side looked tall, Proud Eagle showed Elijah a secret hide out (which is a cave), which could be useful if there was future trouble with the white man. Proud Eagle stopped to rest under the Oak tree. "I'm getting old. Now that you're here, Elijah, I feel so much better, for there are issues that need to be confronted about our people. Time is changing. The young people act like they don't want to stay at the village anymore. Since the Council of Indian Affairs has been helping us, I've been trying to keep everything together. But I don't know how much longer I can do it."

Elijah looks at Proud Eagle with disgust. "I know what you mean. I'm ready to settle down now, so that my lineage can continue to grow like the seeds of life. Come, we must continue on to meet with the Council of Indian Affairs."

Proud Eagle got up from where he was sitting and said, "Yes." We must not be late." Elijah realized what was happening and saw that it would be hard for him. As they walk towards the village, to get through to town, some of the Indians came rushing up to them. "O Great Leader, there was some trouble here." An Indian said, "The Council of Indian Affairs came to see you. They want you come right away."

As the two Great Leaders walked quickly, Snow Feather made sure that Elijah saw her. They finally arrived to the building. The people in the town looked at them, as they were dressed so differently in their buckskin and feathers. Proud Eagle hurried to the office with Elijah right behind him. The Council of Affairs was sitting behind a big large table. As Proud Eagle and Elijah came to present themselves, they sat down in the large, brown leather chairs.

One of them spoke. "Proud Eagle, I'm glad that you could come to this important meeting. It's very important that you know that there is going to be a new development in the area where you have settled. The Building Commission wants to build a college right where you are." There were ten white men on the Council. As Elijah was staring at them, he sensed a wrong feeling that something wasn't going right.

"Proud Eagle, you have been a good citizen dwelling in Tallahassee. We need to come to an agreement right now. Your people can continue to dwell on this land, but it has to be on the other side, west of town." Proud Eagle knew that the other side of town is desolate, with no way to get water and no trees for cover or shade. Proud Eagle held his head down to shake it to and fro.

Proud Eagle got up from the chair to say, "Yes. I've been a good citizen in Tallahassee. It is up to you to help my people get decent housing and resources to continue to live. I'm not going to agree on this matter until you find a better location for my people. Now, as I see it, there is some terrain north of here where there is good vegetation. Why can't I go there?"

The Council took a moment and whispered to one another. One of the Council members looked down at some papers to check for some information... Then the Council members nodded their heads, and one of them finally responded. "Okay. It's agreed that you will settle in the Northwest of town. If you will sign these papers, we can get the development started. When will you be able to move your people?"

Proud Eagle sighed. "Can we have a week?" The Council began to whisper again and nodded their heads yes. "Okay. A week it is." The Council got up for Proud Eagle to sign the papers. Proud Eagle said seriously, "I want a copy of these papers please."

As they shook Proud Eagle's hand, Elijah was stunned to hear what was said. Elijah went to walk out of the room when a Council member walked up to him and asked, "Are you going to be the new leader of this tribe?"

"Yes, I am," Elijah answered sternly. "Remember my face because I have the feeling that you're going to see my face again." The man that spoke to Elijah was a Quinton, and he recalled that they were very prominent in Florida. The Quintons had acquired land all in many locations.

Chapter 2

Conflict Between the Quintons and the Cherokee

The Quintons didn't like Indians and didn't like blacks either. The Quintons and the Williamsons had dwelled in Tallahassee since the early 1700's. They owned Tallahassee. Elton Fitzgerald Quinton was the Sheriff of the town and Barry Williamson was a prominent lawyer. Their families are involved in other civil affairs in the town, and he people in town are very intimidated by them. As Proud Eagle and Elijah walk out of the building, the sun beaming hot and the wind blowing from east to west, Proud Eagle got angry. Elijah didn't say anything, but simply waited for Proud Eagle to say something. Proud Eagle was huffing under his breath as he walked quickly to put some distance between himself and the town. As they were on the trail to get back to the village, Proud Eagle hollers out. "See how the white man is! That Quinton snake! If he wasn't on the

Council, things could be better. Elijah!" Proud Eagle turned to face him and said, "You must promise me that from now, you will not deal with them. I mean it to my grave. Once we leave this time, there is no going back. We will be okay. Our people should be near the secret place that I showed you this morning." As Elijah and Proud Eagle arrived at the village, the people were gathering around waiting to hear what had happened.

Proud Eagle walked slowly towards his people. He looked at them to see what he had to tell them. "We must move." The people start mumbling amongst each other. Proud Eagle raised his hand up to silent them. "What the stupid white man doesn't know is where our secret hiding place is. We won't be too far from it." The people start nodding their heads and smile a little bit. "We have one week to move, and as we move, we will move so fast that they won't know where we went."

One of the Indians asked. "Why do we have to move?" Proud Eagle answered. "They're building a new school called a college near here. Young people, I hope that you will take the advantage of the opportunity to attend this college, because we're going to need some new leaders to guide us and strengthen our tribe in law, medicine, and agriculture."

"I'm telling you my people. Focus on where we are. Yes, Tallahassee is beautiful, but it won't be beautiful, if our lives are ugly. Now, let's start packing the more difficult items. Men, start packing wood and other resources. Women, start packing what you have in your dwelling houses. Young people, help all you can to make it easier for the women."

The Quinton Family

Meanwhile, back at the Court House, Barry Williamson had conversation with Elton Fitzgerald Quinton as they left the Council meeting room. "Well, Elton, we've done it again." Barry chuckled.

Elton shot a very disappointed look at Barry. "Barry, how long are we going to keep making those people suffer?"

Barry returned a frustrated glance at Elton. "As long as I'm living, they'll be alright." Barry pats Elton on the back.

Elton went to his beautiful Victorian home that had six pillars framing his large porch with stained twin glass doors that were decorated with a floral pattern. As he walked into the house, his wife came to greet him with, "Darling, you're just in time for dinner." Elton looked tired. He was thinking about the day's situation with the Indians. Elton replied, "Honey, I'm a little tired. I will be in the den to fix myself a drink."

The wife looked at her husband and saw that he was stressed from the day. "Well, what's the matter?"

"It's those damn Indians and their problems." The wife sighed and walked out of the den to get dinner for the children.

A short time later the rest of the family were waiting to eat their dinner. Elton came into the dining room to greet his children. Jenny, Elsie, and John waited patiently along with their mother at the table for dinner as the black maids were serving them. The wife spoke with a distinctly southern accent to her husband. "Now, Elton, you're not going to spoil your evening thinking about those Indians, are you? I personally hope that they move as far away as possible, if you ask me."

The children looked at their Mother and Father with puzzled expressions on their faces.

Elsie asked, "What's wrong with the Indians? Don't they have the right to live like us?"

This innocent question caused her mother to spit out her drink. Elton's temper flared. "I don't want to talk about this matter anymore, understand?" Everybody went quiet, and dinner continued for the evening.

As the children were getting ready for bed, Elsie said to John, "You know what? I got a feeling that this is not going to be the end of this." Elsie was ten years old, Jenny was eight, and John was twelve. They were smart children, but their parents sheltered them and kept them away from other children. They were even home-schooled by visiting tutors. As they went to bed, the children start thinking about their lives and the Indians' lives, too.

The week had come for the Indians to move off the land that they had lived for quite some time. Elijah, Proud Eagle, and a few other leaders walked in front of the Indian aggregation. They had to settle about thirty miles from where they were. They walked proud, but they didn't beat any drums or sing any hymns. They just wanted to get where they had to go quickly so that they could settle in quickly. Although the trip to the new location was about three hours, they had a lot to pack and load. The women and children had to walk and rest at the same time. The men had to make sure that no one was left behind.

It was early evening when they arrived at the new place. The sun was just going down. The Indians had found that this plot of land was near the river; they began to pitch their dwellings near a small creek that ran through the ravine. The trees were somewhat spread out from each other. Proud Eagle saw that he was going to settle near the secret place and have the rest of his people settle near a large hill so they can get a little shade from the trees. Running Bear and his family settled fifty feet from Proud Eagle.

Elijah liked being near his people, and he looked around for a place for himself. He decided to stake his claim along with Little Feather and his family near the small creek, where there was a small ridge nearby. Proud Eagle said to his people, "Just settle around each other until morning. I assure you that we will be all right." Proud Eagle called for Elijah.

Elijah came to Proud Eagle angry, distraught and restless. Proud Eagle went to embrace Elijah. "Everything is going to be alright, Elijah. By the time the autumn moon comes, we'll be able to get a lot of things done. See you in the morning."

The morning arrived as the sun rose from the East to shine on the Indians. The birds were chirping happily. A hawk flew around the area as Proud Eagle awoke to see it.

Some of the Indians gathered the wood to begin building Proud Eagle's home; rest of the tribe proudly worked to get the task finished so that when evening arrived, they would be ready to settle down. Elijah awoke to see that everybody was getting busy. Little Feathers' people were starting to build Elijah's home. The women were gathering the children together and gave them some dried meat called jerky to eat until they were settled.

Snow Feather looked for Elijah. One of the women caught Snow Feather not paying attention to the job she was supposed to be doing. The Indian woman talked in Cherokee language for Snow Feather to come to help them. Snow Feather caught herself to continue to help the other women.

It was noon. The Indians stopped to rest. Proud Eagle's home was almost finished. The tribe was able to build it quickly with the wood that they had accumulated. Elijah's home was almost finished, too.

Elijah continued to help the others build some small houses for the women and children, but Snow Feather was never too far from his thoughts, and every now and then, he looked around for her, to see where she was. Some of the Indian men went to hunt for food, but they found it difficult to find enough rabbits and squirrels for a meal. They had to go deep into the forest to get them. Everybody was getting frustrated waiting for something to eat.

Chapter 3
Settling in Florida

The Indians were getting restless. They had practically built ten houses as the sun was moving to the West. The men returned in enough time for the women to cook the food hurriedly, for it would be dark soon. The women hurriedly packed their belongings into the houses so that they can put the children to rest. Proud Eagle, Running Bear, Elijah, and Little Feather hurried to place Proud Eagle's belongings into his house.

It was getting into the evening as the sun settled in the West. The Indians gathered around each other to start chanting and praying for the Great Spirit in the Sky to bless them. "We have done well for the day my people. Tomorrow, we'll build protection around this area to show the white man that he can't come here whenever he wants to. Let's go ahead and turn in early, for all of us are tired." Elijah spotted Snow Feather. As he smiled, his eyes invited Snow Feather to come to his house.

Everybody started going to their new dwellings. As Elijah started to go his house, Proud Eagle called for Elijah. Elijah, feeling a bit frustrated, headed toward Proud Eagle's house. As he stepped in, he bowed to him. Proud Eagle had Elijah to sit down. "I know that you're getting frustrated Elijah. Time is pressing on. I know that you're setting your eyes on Snow Feather. Her Father, Big Owl, is a stern old man; I know you've seen him being carried by the young leaders. You're going to have to go to him and ask for Snow Feather very soon."

Elijah replied, "I know this is what I must do. I love her. I need her very much." Proud Eagle got up from his chair with his drink and smiled at Elijah. "I just want you to do the right thing, my son. I'm proud of you Elijah. You have come too far to not have the things you desire in your life. Perhaps when the autumn moon comes, you'll be ready to have Snow Feather as your own." They toasted to each other. Elijah put down his drink and left Proud Eagle's house. As Elijah walked toward his house, Snow Feather showed up to grab Elijah and say, "I've been busy today, but I've been looking for you. Can I stay with you tonight?"

Elijah enjoyed Snow Feather's embrace, but stopped long enough to ask her, "Won't you get in trouble sleeping with me?" Snow Feather replied, "I don't care. I want to be with you Elijah. Don't you understand?"

Elijah was walking toward his house, but he came to a full stop. He to face Snow Feather, grabbed her gently by her arms asked, "What is it Snow Feather? Does your Father want you to marry someone else?"

"No! It's nothing like that, Elijah. I have not placed my eyes on anyone but you Elijah. Please let me stay with you tonight," Snow Feather begged. Elijah sighed as he looks around to see if anyone was watching. The Indians were tired. No one was watching. Not even Proud Eagle. Elijah picked up Snow Feather and carried her into his house. Little Feather had made Elijah a big, four poster bed with soft material made out of rabbit skin to lay her on his bed.

Elijah kissed Snow Feather like he couldn't get enough of her. He stopped to make a fire in the fireplace, and Snow Feather gazed at him as if she were in a trance. Elijah was very handsome. He was tall, with a strong physique, long, black, hair hung down his back, and his shoulders were broad and sculpted.

As he gets the fire going, Elijah turns to smile at Snow Feather. Her teeth shone so bright as she smiled at Elijah and crossed her beautiful, olive-skinned legs. Elijah turned to pick Snow Feather up from the bed to place her on the bearskin rug as he continued to kiss her ears, neck, and throat. Snow Feather pushed her hair back to look at Elijah; his dark eyes glowed like a raving wolf, and she knew he would love her constantly. All night they just held each other without saying anything.

After a while, as they cuddled together, Elijah awoke to see Snow Feather sleeping; to him, she looked like a princess. He covered her up with his Cherokee blanket that he had since his father gave it to him. He held Snow Feather, as he went back to sleep in peace. Morning came. Elijah woke again to discover that Snow Feather was gone. The fire was gone too. He looked outside to see that everybody was still resting. The morning came and left Elijah's house with cool air running through it.

He stared out at the land to see where the mountains and the hills were placed. It was still beautiful to him. They weren't near any palm trees but Elijah didn't care. He'd found a woman and he planned to plant his seed on this ground. As he was admiring the land, and thinking about Snow Feather, Little Feather walked up to ask Elijah how he liked his new home.

Elijah greeted Little Feather like a father greets his son. "Little Feather, how are you this morning?"

Little Feather smiled. "Well, how do you like your new place?"

Elijah answered, "You did a good job Little Feather. I owe you one."

"Proud Eagle sent me to come to get you." Little Feather said. "We got a little more to do." Elijah shut his door to walk with Little Feather. "Yeah, I know. Hey! How do you like your new place?" Elijah asked.

"It's great." Little Feather answered. "I see me as a prospect myself. Snow Feather is beautiful isn't she?" Little Feather asked smiling.

Elijah answered. "Yes she is." Elijah's stride was proud as he went to greet Proud Eagle. Proud Eagle greeted Elijah with a pat on his back. "Come, it's time for you to meet Big Owl. Don't be scared. I'll be right with you." Elijah felt flustered, and he took a deep breath.

The new village was looking half established. The Indians were smiling as Elijah went to see Big Owl. Proud Eagle stepped fast to get to Big Owl's house. "I'm quite sure you had a good night Elijah." Big Owl was sitting on his porch step as the two arrived to see him. Big Owl tried to get up as the men approached, but Proud Eagle waved his hand for him to stay seated. Big Owl's eyesight was failing, and his legs were weak.

"Big Owl, this is one of new leaders that came from the north. He is Elijah, White Cloud's son. You remember Big Owl?"

Big Owl waved his hand for Elijah to come to him. "I've heard so much about you, strong warrior. Perhaps when the autumn moon comes, you will be able to have my Snow Feather. Let's go in to have a smoke."

When Indians came to an agreement amongst themselves, they smoked a strong, herbal substance in a pipe called a Peace Pipe. As the early summer came into the land, the Indians had built their fence around them, established a building where they kept their goods, and constructed another building in which to entertain the little children. Being that they did not have many resources, the female scholars in the tribe would go to the library to get some books for the children to read.

By the end of summer, the Indians had everything they needed to survive. Elijah left for Jacksonville. He went to see about some Indian affairs. He was gone for a month. Snow Feather was pulling her hair out, worrying about her man. Snow Feather didn't know it yet, but when Elijah returned, he would ask for her hand in marriage. He bought her a beautiful, snowy-white Indian dress with rabbit fur fringe around the hem. He also bought her a beautiful white feather headdress, along with an Indian Turquoise necklace and a matching turquoise ring with diamonds surrounding it.

Chapter 4

Elijah Marries Snow Feather

It was getting into Indian summer. The nights were cool, while the days were still hot. As Elijah traveled, he couldn't help thinking about Snow Feather. The huge sun was setting, looking a bright orange. There were no clouds in the sky. Elijah knew that it was time for the big event. He hurried his horse to climb the tall mountain to get across the big river so that he can get home. The Indians at their new village were preparing to gather the harvest they had planted. The older women dressed Elijah's house to prepare him for his marriage to Snow Feather.

Proud Eagle was happy, for he was getting old and tired. He was a good leader to his people. The children would run up to him as if he was Jesus Christ. His thoughts were interrupted by a loud shout. An Indian scout yelled out in

Cherokee that someone was coming. It was Elijah! All the Indians came to greet him. Happily, Snow Feather ran to Elijah as he dismounted his horse, and he turned to pick up his woman and swung her around in front of everybody.

Proud Eagle came through the crowd to greet Elijah with a large embrace. "I'm glad that you've arrived, my son. Come, we must talk about the journey," Proud Eagle said. As the two went into the house, the Indian women came to serve the both of them a hot toddy with some venison loaf. "Well Elijah, tell me, does it look good down there?" Proud Eagle asked.

"Yes!" Elijah replied. "In fact, the weather is better than it is here. The palm trees sway back and forth in the warm breezes. There are fifty Seminoles there. They get a lot of schooling there, too. Because of their great leader, Tecumseh, the Seminoles have influence down there. Maybe in the future, you can talk to your people about these issues."

"Yes. I must do that before I leave this land," Proud Eagle answered. "I know that you're tired. You need to get ready for your wedding tomorrow." The great chief acted as if he didn't want him to leave.

"Good night Proud Eagle," Elijah replied.

Elijah left Proud Eagle smiling like a Cheshire cat. He ran toward his house as Running Bear came running right along with him. "Running Bear, it's good to see you," Elijah said excitedly.

Running Bear stopped running to ask, "Elijah, can we talk?" Running Bear stopped on Elijah's porch to take a deep breath. "I wanted to let you know that you're a good man. I admire you very much. If it is not too much to ask, could my woman and I get married tomorrow with you and Snow Feather?

To Running Bear's astonishment, Elijah let out a whoop; he laughed so loudly and so long that he had to stop and look at Running Bear. "Running Bear, we've come a long way. I do not have any qualms about you and Little Deer sharing our wedding. That is her name, isn't it?"

Running Bear looked flushed. "Thank you, Elijah. You're a true brother in this tribe." They gave each other the Indian handshake, and then Elijah said, "Let's get some sleep. We have a big day tomorrow." As Elijah got in his bed, thoughts about his Snow Feather invaded his mind.

Elijah went into his home and saw how the older Indian women dressed his home with the fruits of autumn upon his fireplace. They dressed his bed with the colors of turquoise beads, and a white panel of curtains to line his four-poster bed, hanging down and waiting for Snow Feather to open them so he could place her in the bed. The fire was burning hungrily.

All Elijah could do was to sit down in his chair to contemplate the wonderful day that would start his new life. Everything was coming before him, as he started to think about what he went through. Elijah reminisced about his Father, White Cloud, and what he went through to get to where he is now. Elijah thought about Lone Eagle. He was told that Lone Wolf had died in a battle in Tennessee. Melancholy began to set in, but he caught himself to realize that he was in his beautiful home looking at the fireplace. He shook himself and got up from his chair. While the owls and the hawks make their night calling, Elijah began to assemble his wedding attire. He had a white tunic and turquoise pants, along with a white and turquoise woven shirt Elijah went back to sleep.

Dawn broke over the camp. The birds were singing, the hawks were swaying, and the eagles were gliding. Elijah awoke and leapt out of bed.

The fire was smoldering in his fireplace and had been since last night. The cold in the room didn't matter to Elijah because he was getting married. At that very moment, someone knocked on the door; it was Little Feather. Little Feather entered the house, saying, "Wow! The tribe has put in much preparation for your wedding, Elijah. I'm so sorry and didn't mean to interrupt you getting dressed."

Elijah looked at Little Feather with so much happiness in his heart. "Little Feather, don't get so excited." Elijah prepares for his wedding. Little Feather looks around Elijah's dwelling and imagined how it would be as a married man. He believed Elijah had special insight, and so he questioned him earnestly.

"Elijah, what does it actually take for a woman to be with you forever?"

Elijah had on half of his attire, but he turned to answer Little Feather. "Little Feather, it takes a lot of moons for a man to know a woman. As the many moons come and go, you will see what kind of woman you need to have. Believe me," Elijah said seriously to Little Feather.

The drums started beating. The Cheyenne Cherokee tribe stepped out in the most wonderful attire that they could find. The young Indians had t positioned Big Owl in front of the canvas to greet his son-in-law and his daughter. The Indians had the children to place beautiful daffodils and morning glories all over the ground. They had decorated the camp elegantly that the Quintons had to come to see.

As Little Feather led Elijah to the wedding, Running Bear greeted them to walk side by side; they strode proudly, for they were about to meet the most beautiful women in the tribe. Meanwhile, Elton and some white men were watching fifty feet from the village. After being spotted, some Indians came to greet them and asked, "Is there a problem, white man?"

Elton got down from his horse to greet the Indian. "No, I heard that the new leader was getting married. We come in peace." The Indians turned to look at each other, and deliberately watched the visitors as they rode away. The drums were beating the wedding song as Snow Feather and Little Deer came walking toward their new husbands. The brides each held bouquets made up of asters, daffodils and magnolias. The women had kept these flowers as they traveled to Florida. They looked at each other, smiling and excited.

As they gathered, Elijah looked at Snow Feather and gasped, seeing how she wore what he bought for her. As the Chief Proud Eagle looked on proudly to engage the wedding, the older women were tearing up and the children was gazing at how beautiful everything was on this day. The wind was blowing softly while the women had their flowers in their hair. Elijah gave Snow Feather a beautiful turquoise and diamond ring. Running Bear gave Little Deer a diamond and topaz ring.

It was October. The sun was big and vibrant. As they kissed each other as man and wife, the Indians cheered in great celebration. The people threw flowers all over them. The older woman directed Snow Feather and Little Deer to sit with Proud Eagle where they had made a tall, wicker chairs like thrones for them to sit like Queens.

The Indians danced all evening. They had deer, buffalo, and rabbit for their repast. They had all kinds of fruit to eat. The children were dancing so happily. Little Feather had found his little girlfriend just to smile at her. As the fabulous four were enjoying themselves dancing, Proud Eagle had tears in his eyes, for he knew that everything was going to be all right.

It was evening. The Indians began to put away the remains of the wedding feast, and they realized that it was time for the couples to be together. The older women took Snow Feather and Little Deer to embrace them. The men shook the hands of Elijah and Running Bear. In Indian tradition, once you're married, the men are supposed to carry their women to their domain.

Elijah couldn't wait to pick up Snow Feather and carry her to his domain. He got half way to put her back down and they both ran to his house. As they got to the house, Elijah picks Snow Feather up to carry her to his domain. Snow Feather laughed with glee when she saw how the older women decorated the place. Snow Feather was so surprised that she turned around to kiss Elijah on his cheek.

Elijah was so pleased that he picked Snow Feather up to put her on his beautiful four-poster bed and kissed her softly. There was food from the wedding feast in the house, but they didn't pay any attention to it. They made love until the birds start singing in the morning.

Chapter 5

Proud Eagle, The Leader of the Cherokee, Dies

Winter had passed. Elijah and Snow Feather were enjoying their lives together. For a period of time, there was peace in the valley. When spring came, Snow Feather was with child. Proud Eagle came down with pneumonia during the hard winter. The older Indians were concerned about his health. Elijah was building a new addition to his house. Running Bear hadn't seen Elijah since early winter. They were very busy taking care of their families. Running Bear went to Elijah to tell him that Proud Eagle was gravely ill. Upon hearing the news, Elijah dropped everything to see about Proud Eagle.

Proud Eagle was bedridden, and the older Indian women were taking care of him. The Indian chief's eyes were shut because of the pain that racked his body. Elijah bent down by Proud Eagle's bed to take his hand and the chief awoke to smile at Elijah. Proud Eagle started to cough violently as he tried to speak. The coughing ceased, and he whispered, "My son, the time has come for me to go to meet my ancestors. Please don't weep." Elijah smiled through his grief, but looked surprised when the chief said, "I may not see your son - yes, you're having a son. However, here's one more thing that you must do before I leave this world. Take ten men to the secret place and show them where I want to be buried. Don't show the women, for they wouldn't understand." Elijah shook his head in assent with Proud Eagle. Elijah arose from kneeling by the bed to leave; he exited the shelter to discover that a few Indians were hanging around the house. Elijah quickly selected from the group ten men that were waiting outside the door. Elijah hung his head sadly and said to the men, "Proud Eagle is dying. We must continue to press on."

One of the Indians asked Elijah. "When Proud Eagle passes away, are we going to move to Jacksonville?"

"It all depends on what the people decide," Elijah answered. "Right now there's nothing we can do. Go to your families, for they need you right now." Elijah returned to his house; he was sad and distraught, but he thought to himself, "It may be a good idea to pack up and leave again. But then again, the white man isn't bothering us. We are at peace right now, but I wonder what they will do once they find out Proud Eagle's dying. I will see first before I make a move."

As spring arrived, Proud Eagle's condition had worsened. The tribe continued living on the land, and the Quintons and the Williamsons continued their observations from afar. They acted very reluctant to talk to Elijah after what they had done to the tribe. Elijah knew that they were being watched, but he didn't want to alarm his people unnecessarily.

The time came. In the beautiful month of April, in the year 1887, as Snow Feather and Elijah delivered their firstborn son, Chief Proud Eagle transitioned from his people. The tribe shed both tears of joy for Elijah's son and tears of sorrow for Proud Eagle's passing. The Cherokee prepared for the chief's funeral.

They burned incense in their houses. They chanted and danced to honor Proud Eagle. Elijah wept as if Proud Eagle was his own Father. Snow Feather had just given birth, but she went to the funeral to console her husband. The people mourned for Proud Eagle for two weeks. All normal activity came to a halt.

They even neglected to be on the lookout for the white man who was watching them constantly. After burying Proud Eagle, Elijah realized that he must talk to the white man about some Indian affairs. Elijah looked at his infant son and named him William. Snow Feather looked on contentedly at the two men in her life. She had no clue what Elijah might have to face in the near future. She went to her husband and asked, "Are you going to be alright?"

Elijah shook his head, disturbed, "I have a feeling that the white man isn't going to stop harassing us. I'm going to talk to them and hope that nothing has changed since Proud Eagle passed away." Snow Feather kissed her husband on his lips, and Elijah held his woman gently by her shoulders. They both started to get aroused, but he stopped and laughingly said, "Hey, that's how we got Will."

Snow Feather told her husband, "I can never get enough of you."

The baby started to cry. As the loving couple stopped their embrace, there was a knock on the door. Elijah opened the door to see that

Little Feather was bleeding like a stuck pig. Snow Feather saw the man and gasped, "I'll get some water!" Elijah picked up the injured man and took him to the sofa. Elijah lightly smacked the half-conscious Indian on his face to get him to come to.

"Little Feather! What happened?" Elijah shouted to his hurt friend.

Little Feather roused himself and finally spoke. "I was fishing down at the meadow when two white men approached me and demanded that I give them the fish that I had caught. When I wouldn't give the fish to them, the men beat me. One of them attacked me from behind; even so, I have no idea who they were." Little Feather's eyes were bruised and his ribs were fractured. Snow Feather brought water and attended to the man's wounds. The bleeding stopped, and Little Feather began to rise from the sofa.

"That's okay Little Feather. I'll get to the bottom of this," Elijah said angrily.

"Oh no, you don't!" said Snow Feather. "Right now, you just lay back down, Little Feather - I need to tend to the baby." She turned and kissed her husband goodbye, a concerned look on her face.

Elijah struck out toward the Podium to get his peoples' attention. He beckoned them to listen, and then he began to speak. "Today Little Feather got attacked by some white men that were passing through. Being that we haven't been watching as we should, we must continue our mission to protect our people."

Chapter 6

Trouble in Florida

As some of the older Indians were nodding their head in agreement, someone in the crowd hollered out, "We ought to move to Jacksonville. You did say that it was better than up here. We're tired of the white mans' foolishness."

Elijah replied, "Now don't be so hasty to move when we just got here. Let me go to them and see what I can do to solve this matter."

Elijah went into town feeling very uneasy. The memory of his last conversation with Elton Quinton made his skin crawl. He knew that Quinton didn't care for the Cherokee Tribe. As he arrived at the Civic Building, Elijah noticed that no one was around. He was walking up the front stairs when he saw Elton exit the building with some businessmen. Elton saw Elijah as he was shaking their hands to part ways with his colleagues.

"Well, if it isn't Elijah, the Great Leader," remarked Elton. What can I do for you?"

Elijah looked at Elton with concern on his face, "I want to know when you're going to have another town meeting."

"Well, Elijah, we just had one," Elton answered. "What seems to be the matter?"

Elijah answered resentfully, "One of the men of my tribe got attacked this morning."

Elton's eyebrows rose up as he listens to Elijah. Elton knew who the culprits were, but he wasn't going to tell Elijah.

"Is that right?" Elton said unconcerned.

Elijah was getting frustrated, "Look! I am trying to talk to you about this matter since you are so concerned. I don't want any trouble. My people have been through enough."

Elton raised his left hand to stop Elijah from saying anymore. "Elijah, I want us to agree on certain matters. Since you're Indian, there's only so much that I can do." He began to walk away dismissively.

Elijah responded angrily. He got in front of Elton, to block his exit. "If I catch any of your men around our grounds - that's right, OUR grounds - you'll be very sorry, because I've warned you. Do you see any of my people trying to go to the theatres around here? Or, shall I say, knocking on YOUR door for anything? You shun us as if we are poison, but you come lurking around our camp like a sneaky weasel. What is it, Elton? Don't you have enough guts to tell your people to stay away from my people?"

By the time Elijah finished, Elton's face was red. Elton walked away without saying a word. Elijah watched him retreat down the street. When Elijah returned to the settlement, the people gathered around him expectantly.

Elijah says, "As you know, its' going to be a very hot summer. How many of you want to move to Jacksonville?"

Only half of the young Indians raised their hands and the older Indians kept their hands down.

One of the young Indians protested, "It would be better for us young generation to move out because we need an education, and we can't sit around here waiting for something to happen. We need to make something happen." The Cherokee Tribe realized that things were changing quickly.

Elijah did not want to leave Tallahassee. He planned to have more children with his wife in the place where they were, but there were too many challenges for the tribe. The younger Cherokee women were given a hard time when they went to the library to get supplies for their children. Elijah knew that he would have to go into town to tell the white folks that not everything was theirs.

Running Bear was aging and he was tired of having to face the same issues over and over again.

Meanwhile, Little Feather had regained consciousness. He walked outside to the news that the younger group wanted to go to Jacksonville. Little Feather said. "I, Little Feather, will be glad to take the younger generation to Jacksonville."

The young Indians gave Little Feather a pat on the back because they wanted a change in their lives. Snow Feather walked out onto the porch and beckoned Little Feather to return to the house to rest.

Elijah returned to the village to find out the news of the younger Indians wanting to leave for Jacksonville and that Little Feather wanted to take them. Elijah gets to his home to see that Little Feather and his son were asleep. Elijah found Snow Feather crying while she was cooking dinner; Elijah goes to her to ask what was wrong.

"My father is dying, and Little Feather wants to take the younger generation to Jacksonville," Snow Feather said.

Elijah pulled Snow Feather into a tight embrace. "Don't cry, Snow Feather. We will work this out. Whatever happens, we must stay together to care for the elders in the tribe."

Little Feather awoke to see Elijah. "I guess you've heard, huh?" Elijah nodded his head and put his hand on Little Feather's shoulder. "I understand, Little Feather, how you young ones feel being here," Elijah replied sadly.

It was summer time. The weather was very hot and balmy. Snow Feather's father passed away. The funeral was long and sad. The young Indians were packing to leave for Jacksonville. As the older Indians embraced their children and bid them farewell, Little Feather went to Snow Feather and baby William to get his last hug. The baby loved Little Feather, and showed it by gurgling and slobbered all over Little Feather's face.

Elijah told his people to stay focused on their future plans and be careful on their new journey. Little Feather and thirty young Indians struck out on their journey to a new life. Elijah gazed after his young people on top of the hill by his house, as Snow Feather held her husband around his waist with their son and waved goodbye to Little Feather.

Time passed and the Cherokee tribe was growing rapidly. Since Proud Eagle's death, there was some happiness for once - Running Bear had two sets of twins. Soon after, Elijah and Snow Feather came to expect another child. William was now seven years old and Elijah taught his son how to hunt, navigate, and learn about herbs on the earthy grounds. Years went by and Snow Feather had four more children: Gene, Hilda, George, and Matilda.

Even though the younger generation left the village, the Cherokee nation stood with pride and dignity. The Quintons watched as Elijah and his generation grew in the new decade. The Indians still were not allowed to go to the white man's movies nor functions. However, the Indians had their own entertainment. Five years went by without Elijah having any contact with Elton Quinton. In spite of the time, the two men still knew that one day they would have to deal with one another. Elton's son John was almost out of middle grades and he and Elijah's son, William would sneak and play with each other after school faithfully.

Elton taught John racism, prejudice, and hate, but John was quite interested in dealing with Indians the same way his father did. He had a good heart. The ideas that John's father taught him were ignorant and bitter. Elton's son stayed under his mother. His mother gave John a positive outlook with a warm nurturing touch. His sisters Jenny and Elsie were very sheltered. Their mother would not let them play with other middle-class children.

In the winter of 1897, as the leaves stopped falling to make the trees bare and desolate, Snow Feather became pregnant for the sixth time. It was a bitter, cold winter. The Cherokee were having a hard time making it through because they had to cut so many trees to keep them warm. Elijah realized that the new addition to the house was not large enough for his children. Therefore, he built another fireplace in the room addition to keep all of his children warm.

Chapter 7

Susie Poohtawn is Born

It was close to Christmas. Snow Feather was dropping heavily, for the baby was about to arrive. Her eldest children helped her out a lot around the house. Snow Feather would read stories to her children about Pocahontas and Sacajawea, the Indian women that helped white men in this country. She showed them how to cook and to gather nuts and berries for Christmas decorations. This particular year Snow Feather was having a difficult pregnancy. She was always more tired than usual and extremely irritable. Sometimes, the older Cherokee women would come to help her out in her discomfort.

Christmas came. Susie Poohtawn, to the woman who would be my great-grandmother, was born. She looked just like her father. She had coal black, wavy hair. She had her father's nose and

83

his eyes. The only characteristic that she had of her mother's was her infectious smile. The older children spoiled little Susie all winter long. By the time spring came, her knee baby sister Matilda and Susie became very close.

The weather was nice and cool. The sky was purple and blue with cirrus clouds swirling in the air. On this day, Snow Feather had her children out for some air because the winter had been very harsh. A few of the elder Indians had died during the past winter. All of the women were out and milling about enjoying the day. It was during that time when Little Feather came home to visit his family. He was amazed to see that Elijah had many children. Little Feather especially took a liking to Susie, the baby girl.

Little Feather saw that Susie looked like her father. Her hair was long and wavy. She walked toward Little Feather so he could pick her up. He held her in his arms while Snow Feather and the other women were preparing dinner. As she smiled at Little Feather, he could see that Susie's little jawbones were strong and vibrant. After the family had dinner, Running Bear came over to spend some time with Elijah and Little Feather. Elijah sat down in his favorite chair to talk with his favorite brothers in the tribe.

"Time surely is passing by," Elijah laughs as they talk about their children and the issues that they had with the white man. Little Feather still did not have any children.

Running Bear asked, "Little Feather, when are you going to settle down?"

Little Feather sighed and said, "I'm not ready. There's too much going on right now in Jacksonville with the young tribe."

Elijah asks, "What's going on?"

"Well, the system has it that they don't want us to go to school with the other children of color, but there is an overseer that's helping us. As I hear it, this William McKinley, the President is not doing anything to help the fellow man. Why is it Elijah, Our Great One, that these leaders in the States won't help us?"

Elijah answered, "Listen to me. Even though my time will come to leave this earth, you can be sure of this, the white man is going to continue to destroy all that he owns."

"At the time of Custer, my granddaddy told me stories how this President William H. Harrison who took our land to make the railroad. An Indian Chief had a twin brother that predicted the fate of every president within twenty years that would die. So what I am telling you is to keep on fighting for what's right, because the Great Spirit in the Sky will always look out for you. Go back to Jacksonville to tell our people to hold their head up and continue to fight for their cause."

Running Bear stood up to praise. He shook his head with so much excitement when suddenly his wife called him, "I must go now, but Little Feather, listen to Elijah."

He grabbed Little Feather to say goodbye in his native Indian language. "Don't forget that ever!"

"I won't Running Bear," Little Feather had a tear in his eye as he watched Running Bear leave them.

Elijah grabbed Little Feather by his shoulder as they walked toward the house. "You're leaving tomorrow?"

Little Feather answered, "Yes! I'm ready now."

"Good," Elijah replied.

The evening settled in. It was a quiet evening. The children were getting sleepy, all of them except for little Susie. She wanted to stay up with her parents and Little Feather. Little Feather was enjoying playing with the child. Snow Feather eventually came to get her little girl to put her to bed, but Susie started crying because she did not want to go to sleep.

"Da-da," she said, holding her arms out for her father. Elijah took her into his arms and tried to rock her to sleep.

Little Feather remarked, "She's spoiled."

Snow Feather replied. "Yes, she's spoiled, and it's her father's fault." Elijah ignored the remarks while pacing the room and softly singing some Indian lullabies to his daughter. Susie went to sleep peacefully.

"I think we all should get some sleep," said Elijah.

Little Feather went straight to his favorite spot where he liked to sleep. Elijah and Snow Feather bade their friend good night and went to bed.

It seemed that the morning came quickly. Snow Feather arose early to fix breakfast and to prepare Little Feather for his journey. The older Indians got up from their slumber and came to say goodbye to Little Feather. William was on the porch near tears, because he loved Little Feather so dearly. Little Feather taught William a lot about the land and about being an Indian. As William was crying, Little Feather walked up to William and told him, "Be strong William. I'll be back to see you."

"Okay. You had better come back, Little Feather. I'm going to hold you to that." William held on to Little Feather, not wanting to let him go.

"Come Son. Little Feather has to get going." Elijah said sadly. He and his son watched Little Feather as he mounted his horse and rode out of the settlement as everybody waved goodbye. The rest of the children awoke to discover Little Feather had left, and began to cry. Elijah went to his children to embrace them, but assured them that one day Little Feather would be back.

It was 1901. Teddy Roosevelt became President. Some things started to change when it came to Indian Affairs. President Roosevelt made sure that he kept the environment clean in the nation, and yet he collected many animals he had hunted and placed them on the walls in his home. The United States became engaged in what would be called the 'Spanish-American War.' He also called the "Buffalo Soldiers" to help him out while he was away.

My great-grandmother was four years old. She was fat and healthy for her age. There were many changes occurring within the camp. Snow Feather was getting older and tired. Susie's two brothers George and Gene moved away to Louisville, Kentucky. They would never move back to Tallahassee. Elijah was very disappointed and he worried about the rest of his children. The older Indians were dying off one by one. Running

Bear continued to persevere and over time, Snow Feather became ill.

The Quinton Family

During this time, the Williamsons and the Quintons were gaining strength in political offices. Elton backed off from bothering Elijah and it had been years since their last confrontation. While his family grew right in front of his eyes, Elton had no clue that his children, John and Elsie, were secretly playing with Elijah's children, William, Susie, and Matilda. Hilda stayed off to herself. Matilda and Hilda did not get along anyway. Hilda would cause problems with her other siblings and had grown very unhappy since her other two brothers moved away to Louisville.

Meanwhile, Mother Quinton had little to do with her own children. She left the black maids to raise them. Because the maids were so nurturing, Elsie took to them instead of her own mother. Mother Quinton, in turn, spent a lot of time drinking. Elton was never at home, so she turned to the bottle.

Matilda eventually took a liking to a near-college-age John Quinton. The two of them would meet in the woods to play "Hide and Go Seek." John also spent time fishing with William while the girls would distract them.

Elijah knew the children would spent time together. He just didn't make a big deal out of it. He was busy taking care of other affairs in the tribe. Elijah would confide in Running Bear about what was going on, in the event something were to happen to them. Snow Feather's condition would worsen. He called for the elderly women to come to help her get well. They tried everything to treat her, from the Native American herbs to the white man's medicine.

Elijah called for his children to talk to them about their mother's imminent passing. Gene and George received word about the illness and came back to see their mother. While back in Tallahassee, Gene had a major disagreement with his father about William. As it happened, George followed Gene in everything he thought and did. It did not matter how differently Elijah had raised William from Gene and George. The boys knew that Snow Feather, however, had loved and treated all of her children just the same.

One day, Elijah was sitting on his porch smoking his pipe. All three of his sons came out to talk to their father.

"Father, we know that it's been hard for you." Gene said sadly. "I'm sorry that I caused you problems." George nodded his head in agreement.

William stood up before his brothers - his black curly hair locked with an Indian band around his head – and said to them, "You two are my brothers. We don't have time for such resentment. If you're going back to Louisville, then go! The rest of the family here will be fine! Little Feather will be back. As far as I'm concerned, He's my brother!"

Embarrassed and ashamed, Gene and George looked at each other. George tried to embrace William, but William snatched away from him to walk away from the group.

Elijah said, "That's enough! William, come back here! Let me tell you something. I know that it's been rough. I love you all, you, Gene and George! I know that you want to see me proud of you, and I am! Whether you want to live here with the family or away on your own, you need to know that I'm still proud of you."

Just then, the Medicine Man who had been treating Snow Feather, came out of the house and told Elijah that there is nothing else that could be done for his wife. Everybody began to weep at the news. Elijah jumped up to go to Snow Feather. As he approached the bedroom, Snow Feather's long gray hair was brittle and dry. Her eyes were closed shut, but she felt her husband's presence as he entered the room. She turned her head towards him, and Elijah took her hand into his.

"I love you. You know that, don't you? Please take care of Susie. Get one of the elders to take care of her." Snow Feather was in tears as she opened her eyes to look at her husband. "Send my children in here to me, my love."

Elijah wept. He kissed her on her hands and her head, and held her in his arms for a brief moment before he pulled himself away to get the rest of the children. As Elijah got up and let go of his wife's hands, she closed her eyes again.

Elijah went to get the children. Matilda was hysterical at the thought of her mother's passing, but Elijah had to console her and told her to be strong while she went to talk with their dying mother. As the children surrounded the bed, Snow Feather opened her eyes again to look at her children. She smiled at them as she whispered, "Take care of your father. He's going to miss me very much." William especially nodded his head earnestly, and Hilda looked on solemnly. "I love you all," she whispered again, and then took her last breath.

"Mama!" William and Matilda said together. Gene moved to Susie to hold her up because she was about to faint. In fact, all the Indians mourned loudly at the news of Snow Feather's transition. Running Bear sent word of the passing to Little Feather so that he could bring some of the younger generation of the tribe to the funeral.

Elijah took a walk into the forest to where he and Snow Feather would occasionally go and spend time together. He needed to burn a fire and be with his wife in spirit.

"My dear wife," Elijah spoke over the flames, "I will be with you soon. Since you came into my life, you gave my life beauty, purpose and a sense of well-being. I thank the Great Spirit for sending you to me. Life is gone out of me now. I must stay strong until my time comes." Elijah threw some dust into the fire for the fire to burst with beautiful colors of white, green, blue, and red. He just stared at the fire until it burned itself out.

The morning came, gloomy and sad. Little Feather, having missed the train, eventually arrived at the settlement. He went straight to Elijah, and they cried in each other's arms. Gene and George walked up to Little Feather to shake his hand. Little Feather was glad to see them.

Everybody was preparing for the funeral. The girls were about to get dressed when Matilda asked Hilda if she going to be all right. Hilda coldly replied, "I'll be fine."

Matilda looked at her sister to shake her head. "Mama loved you too, Hilda." Hilda just ignored her sister as she continued to dress herself for the funeral.

When Snow Feather had her second child, Hilda, she entered the world with a negative attitude. Snow Feather gave her son George the responsibility of tending to his sister. It was as if Hilda did not want her own mother to take care of her. However, when Snow Feather had Matilda, Hilda began to feel unloved and pushed to the side. Therefore, she clung to her father. Elijah gave Hilda his attention, because he felt that if he did not love her, no one else would. After they buried their mother, the children held onto each other for dear life as they walked back to the house for the evening meal. Little Feather held onto Susie. Susie just blushed and was very glad to see Little Feather. Matilda and Hilda each wore bleak expressions. Matilda smiled through her grief, but Hilda looked on everyone with resentment. Everybody gathered around the home, but they kept a close eye on Elijah as he went into his bedroom to lie down.

The men were all on the porch talking and reminiscing about their lives in Tallahassee. They were talking about how they had to learn how to hunt, navigate, and ride the horses on the plains. They talked about the whippings that they had gotten with Running Bear's children. Meanwhile, Running Bear was in the bedroom with Elijah as they listened to their children talk.

The old men laughed to themselves. Elijah got up from his bed. "You know what Running Bear? This is what I miss. All of us being together, having a good time with our children. I am going to be all right. I have these children to look after and Susie looks just like my wife. I have a distinctive feeling that she's going to break my heart."

"Aww, come on, Elijah." Running Bear replied. "She'll be alright."

Elijah said reluctantly, "Not with that white boy, she won't."

The day finally came when George and Gene would depart to return to their homes. Little Feather and the young tribe would leave for Jacksonville, also. Little Feather managed to catch Susie by herself. He observed that she had grown into a beautiful young woman. He went up to her and said, "Susie, I think you are the most beautiful girl that I've ever seen. I know that I am too old for you, but if there is anything that I can ever do for you, you let me know. Understood?" Susie was stunned, and at a loss for words.

"Little Feather, I looked up to you as if you're my brother." She held him to tell him that she missed him.

She returned his intense gaze and said, "I appreciate that, Little Feather." Susie looked at him as if she could be with Little Feather. Susie hugged her brothers goodbye and watched them leave. Hilda cried for the first time and Matilda embraced her sister.

A few weeks went by and John hadn't come visit William in a long time. William was growing into a tall, handsome man. John had been tutoring William during some of their time together. Susie was also waiting for John to come. Susie asked William if he had seen John recently.

William replied, "No, I haven't seen him. I wonder what is going on. I think I have an idea. I'll be back."

Elijah was busy moving furniture around the house since Snow Feather had passed. William went into town and discovered that John was going away. The maids were helping John to pack when William approached. John looked sad when he told William that he was about to leave for college and he would be back in two years.

"Tell Susie that I'm sorry that I have to leave so suddenly," said John. "I'm going to miss her terribly."

William asked, "What are you going to college for?"

John replied, "I'm going to be a Lawyer."

"Oh!" William looked puzzled.

John told him to go a white man named Mr. Nelson. "He will take care of you as far as your education. Oh, and Elsie has been asking about you. Take care of my sister for me, and Jenny. Goodbye William."

William didn't hear from John for a long time. In the meantime, Susie grew up to be a strong, vibrant young lady. William took John's direction and went to Mr. Nelson for ongoing education. Elijah was getting old, and Running Bear was too. There were very strong men who managed the tribe and Elijah's daughters took care of the house. Hilda kept to herself much of the time, constantly thinking about going to Louisville, Kentucky to be with her brothers George and Gene.

It was midwinter. Matilda got sick with pneumonia. Elijah was at his wits end. He just lost his wife, and now one of his children was terminally ill. Needless to say, it broke Hilda's heart to know that her sister was dying. Susie felt so alone that she clung to another Indian sister in the tribe because she was never close to Hilda. Elsie would sneak over to come to play with her new friend, but it was not the same since John left.

Matilda died in the early spring. Elijah decided to move out of the house to find himself a smaller dwelling in which to live. William eventually left the village to sow his oats. He moved into town so that he could get to the resources that he needed. He stayed close by his family in case they needed him. One of the older Indian women would tend to Elijah, for he was getting old.

Elsie came to see Susie one day, and found her crying. It seemed that Jenny started seeing a black man, but their daddy found out and killed him right in front of the house. This was not before the man had gotten Jenny pregnant, and they sent her off to an insane asylum.

"What am I going to do?" Elsie cried to Susie. "John isn't here right now, but he will be here soon."

"When is he coming?" Susie asked.

Elsie looked at Susie and answered, "Oh, John will be home this summer. I'll be glad when he comes home."

"I'll be glad when he comes home too," Susie replied.

While John was gone, Susie started helping her people with civil affairs in the village. Elsie started to help acquire supplies for the young people as well. Since their mother was gone, Hilda started going to town to seek after her own pleasure. Elijah left her to her own devices, because since her sister Matilda died, he could not control her anymore.

Chapter 8

Susie Grows Up

My grandmother Susie would go to town wearing her long, Victorian dress made with lace on the shoulders, carrying her lace parasol over her head. The white women would watch Susie, as she would strut down the street. They envied her. Susie did not care what they thought. Little did they know that John Quinton was her man and there was nothing that they could do about it.

My great-grandmother was a sharp, fancy lady. She wore those ten-hole boots that laced up to her ankle. Elsie would be walking right alongside her. Elsie missed her sister Jenny. It was like that she would never see her again. Hilda didn't care too much for Elsie, because she was rich.

When Elsie try to speak to Hilda in town, Hilda would turn around and go in another direction. Elsie knew what Hilda was doing, but she did not make a big deal out of it, because she knew what kind of woman Hilda was. As the evening came for them to depart, Susie asked Elsie a question. "Elsie, if John and I wind up getting married, you wouldn't tell your mother that we knew each other, would you?"

Elsie replied, "Oh no! I would not dare tell Mother nor Father. I know that our fathers cannot stand each other. But it's been years since I've heard anything about your father and mine."

Susie smiled. "Good! So, when I come up in your family's house, you'll pretend like you don't know me, right?"

Elsie crossed her heart with her fingers, "Right."

As Susie left Elsie to return to the village, Susie started thinking about Little Feather and what he would say if he was to see her now. Thinking about her brothers and sisters, Susie knew that it was now up to her to keep things straight with her father. Susie loved her father Elijah. She really did not want to disappoint him, but she was afraid that she would.

As soon as Susie arrived at the house, her heart sank. She saw that her father's home was a mess, and cleaning had not happened in a while. Elijah was lost without his Snow Feather taking care of things. Lately her father had been spending a lot of time in his room, and only coming out to eat. He had become withdrawn and not very talkative lately. Running Bear would come to see him every now and then.

Susie shook her head, and was about to start cleaning up when someone knocked at the door. It was William. Susie hugged her brother. "How are you Susie?"

"William! I'm so glad to see you!"

William looked around the house, saw its sorry condition, and asked his sister, "What's going on, Susie?"

Susie explained to William that Hilda hardly comes home to see about them. "Daddy doesn't seem to have any life in him anymore."

William asked, "Where is he?"

Susie pointed at the door to her father's room. William opened the door; the room was dark because the windows were covered, but the unusual odor that came from his bedroom was overwhelming.

"Dad, what are you doing in the dark?" William went for the window.

"Don't open those curtains!" Elijah hollered out.

"Come on Dad," William said with concern. "You have to pull yourself out of this. Mama has been gone for quite some time now. There are some other Indian women in the tribe who would to be glad to take care of you." William partially uncovered a window that allowed enough light into the room so that he could see his father laying on the bed. Elijah's hair was beautifully gray. His eyebrows and his beard was pure white.

Elijah answered his son. "I don't want those women coming here anymore. Running Bear's fat-assed cousin tried to make a pass at me last week. I ran her ass out of here."

William laughed aloud. "Aww, come on Dad, it can't be that bad." Elijah rolled his eyes at William and turned his head away from him.

William said, "Dad, I only came by to see how you're doing. I know that I have been busy. I will tell you what. I have heard from Little Feather. He's doing okay."

Elijah sat up in his bed to listen. "How's my boy doing? I miss that boy."

William looked at the bedroom to see his mother's belongings in the bedroom were gone. "Little Feather said that he'll be here soon." William said.

Elijah chuckled and said, "He thinks he's coming for Susie, but Susie likes that white boy. But we all know that I hate his Daddy, that Elton son-of-a – !"

"Dad!" William cuts in to say. "Dad, I've been finding out that those Williamsons and those Quintons are lynching black men for no reason.

"Oh! Great Father!" Elijah grabs his hands together. "William, you must see to it that my Susie doesn't get to that boy. I heard that he's coming home soon."

"Dad, I'll do my best," said his son.

Elijah laid back down. "I know that you have been friends with that boy since you all were kids. I didn't say anything because you are a boy. But when it comes to my Susie, I can't handle it."

Susie was listening at the door. She already had some rabbit stew bubbling in the fireplace. As she waited for William to come out of her father's bedroom, she started to cry. Hell, she kept reading about the Indian women named Sacajawea and Pocahontas. They married white men so why couldn't she? It was obvious that these fine women helped their men through the toils and snares of life and so would she.

Yeah, yeah, yeah, they went through some pain. It didn't stop them for loving their men to get through history's courses of life. She thought about Elsie. Elsie encouraged her to read about different people. She had this on her mind when William came out of the bedroom. He realized that Susie had heard everything that was said. She grabbed William to sob on his shoulder. William just hugged his baby sister, rubbing her back, telling her to let it all out.

"Listen to me, my sister," said her big brother. "I know love goes a long way. Little Feather will be here soon." Susie's eyes got big, and she stopped crying. As she wiped her tears on her apron, Susie looked at William and told him what Little Feather said to her when their mother died.

"Well, Susie, why don't you?" William asked.

"William, I love John!" Susie exclaimed. She shook her head and attempted to change the subject. "Why don't you stay for dinner?"

William looked around the messy house again. He reluctantly answered, "No. I have some things to take care of." William embraced his sister and looked her in her eyes. "Be strong Susie." She nodded to let him go to the door.

"William!" As he turned around, Susie said, "Don't stay away so long."

"I won't," he replied. "I love you, little sister." As Susie watched her brother leave, she shut the door behind him. She realized that in order to feed her Daddy, she to go into that foul-smelling room to serve him some rabbit stew.

Chapter 9

Troubled Hilda

William went back into town to look for Hilda. He was steaming mad. He had been told that Hilda was selling herself to those rich men at some parlor in town. As he approached town, people were walking along the street laughing and having a good time. The part of town that Hilda was hanging around was very depressed. It had those small houses that resembled shacks from the slavery days, but had an illusion of fences surrounding their houses with flowers and bushes.

He got out of his horse and buggy to enter the parlor where Hilda was supposed to be staying. He heard familiar sounding laughter and a voice that sounded like his sister. He peeped into the window to see that it was Hilda. She was sitting in the lap of Elton Quinton. He turned his head from the window to take a deep breath. William's heart was beating fast. As he tried to catch his breath, he saw his sister go with Elton up the stairs to accommodate him.

William gathered himself and walked into the parlor as if he hadn't seen anything. The Madam approached him and asked, "May I help you?"

William answered the Madam. "My sister Hilda, I was told that she stays with you."

The Madam raised her eyebrows, "What do you want from me?"

William took the woman by her arm. "I want you to get my sister from that Elton guy right now!" William pulled out twenty dollars to give to her.

The Madam went upstairs hurriedly to knock on the door. Elton hollered out, "Who is it?"

"It's the Madam of the house." The Madam waited for him to come to the door. Hilda was busy undressing. Elton opened the door and the Madam saw that he was half-dressed.

"There seems to be a problem," the woman told Elton. "Hilda needs to come downstairs right away."

Elton hollered. "I paid my money for some service, and you mean to tell me that there is a problem?"

The Madam said, "I will surely pay you for your inconvenience. Hilda, get dressed." Hilda looked confused, not knowing what was happening, but she put her clothes back on. Elton angrily looking at her and wondering what was going on. As Hilda descended the stairs, she saw William standing there, looking angry like her father. Whenever William got angry, his eyes turned red as fire like a wolf.

As Hilda sees her brother's eyes, she turned to go back upstairs. The Madam got out of their way. William grabbed Hilda by the arm to take her out of the parlor. By that time, Elton called for the Madam to give him someone else.

William slammed the door behind him so that he could talk to Hilda outside. "What in the hell do you think you're doing, Hilda? You're needed at home!"

Hilda snatched her arm away from William. "I'm not ever going back there! You all didn't give a damn about me!"

William snatched her again. "Let me tell you something, Hilda. You are my sister, too and I'm not going to allow you to do things that you are going to regret later in your life! Since Mama and Matilda died, you've changed! You act as if you didn't give a damn about Matilda dying and you treat Susie as if she's nothing to you. Susie needs you. I went by the house today. Daddy is holed up in his room like some crazy man. Hilda, they need you, so I'm taking you back home!"

Hilda began to cry. She allowed her brother to put her in the buggy. She managed to collect herself and took a deep breath to say, "I didn't think you cared, William. You know that Susie is Daddy's favorite because she looks so much like him." The fact was that Hilda was not a bad-looking woman. Both Matilda and Hilda inherited their looks from their mother, so they were both beautiful.

The horses pulled the buggy forward as William replied to Hilda. "Hilda, I know it's rough. I'm trying to establish some business so that I can watch those Quintons and Williamsons.

"You come from the Cherokee tribe and we are a proud people, too! You need to realize and understand that your time will come. Quit rushing things. If you want me to get you someone, I will. However, right now, you need to be with Daddy and Susie at the house. I know it is hard. I see how things are. Little Feather is on his way back home and some of the women from the village have been asking about you.

"You know Running Bear's Auntie loves you. If you don't want to stay at the house, Sashan said that you could stay with her. Her husband died last winter; she needs someone to be with her. You can do this, Hilda, because I know that you and Susie are going to wind up being together in the end."

"How do you know these things William?" Hilda asked puzzled.

William replied. "You seem to forget Hilda; I'm a bona fide Cherokee."

Hilda sighed and said, "Okay William, I'm going to do right. Can I ask you something? What does Susie want with that white boy?" Hilda took a moment to reflect, and said, "I remember you playing with him, but Susie was just a toddler then."

William explained, "Yeah, but as we played together, Susie saw John and her whole world changed. No one paid attention to it, but I did."

As William got back to the house, the light was on for Hilda. "Now remember, you know how to reach me. Go in there with a good attitude, Hilda, because Susie has gotten to be a strong woman now. Look after Daddy. You know he misses you." William kissed his sister on the head.

Susie said, "William, I'm glad you rescued me tonight. I really didn't want to do that."

William smiled. Susie opened the door to greet her sister.

"Hilda, where have you been at, girl?" Susie yelled back in toward Elijah's bedroom. "Daddy! Daddy! Hilda's here!"

Before Hilda could say anything, Elijah came out of the bedroom to say. "I know what you've been doing, Hilda. How dare you allow white men to touch you?"

Susie looked shocked. Hilda looked at her Daddy, "Daddy, I'm sorry that I've caused you pain. I know that I should be here helping our people get by."

"Get by?" Elijah interrupted. "Let me tell you something," he said as he went to grab a skillet out of the kitchen. "Susie has been helping the young children to read and to handle other affairs in this village. It seems that you have just been waiting to see how much money you can get. It is not all about that, Hilda! You are my daughter, too, and you are to be here for as long as Susie is here. Do you understand me?"

Elijah's aging eyes remained a pale blue; they no longer glowed red when he got angry. He dropped the skillet on the floor, went back to his room and slammed the door. The girls looked at each other in stunned silence and then started laughing. They went outside on the porch to look at each other as if they were strangers. Susie sighed and said to Hilda, "I know that you're older than me, but there is a lot of things that I must say to you.

"Hilda, I didn't realize that you liked Little Feather. Hell, I am the baby of the family, and a whole lot has happened since Mama passed. All we have is each other. Have you heard from Gene and George?"

Hilda shook her head to say no.

"I didn't think you had. William is our oldest brother," Susie continued. "He's got to get his life together like everybody else. If you just wait and pray to the Great Spirit, He will answer our prayers."

Hilda waited for her sister to finish talking so that she could speak. She crossed her legs and said, "So, I've heard that you got your eyes set on John Quinton."

Susie suddenly looked flushed, but answered honestly. "Yes, I do have my eyes on him."

Hilda responded, "Don't you know that Daddy can't stand his father, Susie?"

Susie looked pained at the knowledge, but answered Hilda. "Yeah, I know. You know what, Hilda? I see that since I've been born, I have been reading many books about our ancestors. They had it hard. You ought to be ashamed of yourself for not knowing this. I mean, well, not realizing that we have to be strong women. You know that white men look at us like we ain't shit. Well, I've been walking around downtown like I own it. I walk with dignity and courage. Hilda, you've got to feel the same way too."

As the owls were hooting, and the fireflies were dancing around the bushes, Hilda looked at her sister and said, "When the elder women were trying to get me to read, I would play like I had something else better to do. Susie, I think you were right, because I see now that I know that we're not going to be here long. My revelation is coming to me, too, because I am a Cherokee, and I'm going to make sure that we stay together."

Elijah hollered to his girls from inside the house. "Y'all come on in here. There's a big day tomorrow." The girls looked at each other laughing, as they held each other to go back inside that mess of a house. Hilda and Susie began to prepare for bed. Before they turned in for the night, they cleaned up the kitchen and found some incense to burn. They burned it both to honor the memory of their mother, and to get that awful smell out of the house.

Things started to get better. Susie and Hilda were getting along just fine. The house started to look better as they waited for Little Feather to come home. William was coming by the house frequently. Daddy Elijah was coming out of himself to spend time with the old Indian men in the village. Susie hadn't seen Elsie in a while. She started to think about their last conversation. One day, Hilda was in the front yard putting some flowers in the yard when all of a sudden, she saw Little Feather coming in his horse and buggy. Hilda dropped everything she was doing and yelled out, "Little Feather is here!" At the time, Susie was in the bedroom helping her father get dressed. Elijah didn't give Susie a chance to do his hair, but moved past Susie in order to get to the door to greet Little Feather.

As Little Feather approached the house, Elijah's daughters had not seen him display such energy in a long as he did approaching Little Feather. Elijah grabbed Little Feather and started to cry. Little Feather had always been slim. His height emphasized his strength and his shoulders had grown muscular and developed. The girls stood on the porch watching their father and his friend happily.

Their Daddy had come alive since he heard Little Feather was coming home. Little Feather's age had brought him finesse and beauty in an Indian man. Susie remembered his proposition to her. Little Feather grabbed Hilda into hug and she blushed warmly. Hilda shot a look at Susie to see if she was jealous. Susie wasn't jealous; she was already aware of Little Feather's affections toward her.

Little Feather then embraced Susie. "Hello, Susie. It's so good to see you." As he let her go from his strong arms, Susie almost melted, but she kept her composure in front of her father and Hilda. Little Feather's gaze upon Susie was so warm and intense that she almost missed a step as she walked up on the porch.

Both Hilda and Elijah started to laugh. They all sat down on the porch decorated with a variety of flowers, which included black-eyed Susans, daffodils, and pink and orange pansies, with magnolias hanging from the porch ceiling. The day was warm, and the rest of the Indians were very happy that Little Feather was home. After they finished eating supper, they returned to the porch to discuss all of the events that had happened since Little Feather's departure.

"A lot is happening in Jacksonville. Everybody is doing well. Many young people have finished their education, received their degrees and have moved on."

Elijah smiled and nodded. "I'm glad that things worked out for our people." Everybody was celebrating the return of Little Feather, but Hilda remained quiet, not wanting any attention drawn to herself and trying to avoid answering any personal questions. However, Little Feather finally looked at Hilda and addressed her. "Hilda, I know that you've been doing some things since I've been gone."

Elijah, Susie, and Hilda looked at one another to hear what Hilda was going to say. Hilda's reluctance and discomfort were obvious through her stammering. "I – uh –"

Susie jumped in to rescue her sister. "Hilda has been helping me with some civil affairs in the village."

Hilda sighed and smiled. "Yes, that's exactly right. That's what I've been doing." Elijah had been holding his head down; at the answer from his daughters, he raised it up with a smile. Little Feather then asked Elijah, "Where's William?"

Susie answered for her father. "He'll be here soon." Once Little Feather's gaze was directed back to Susie, he couldn't take his eyes off her.

Elijah jumped in and said, "Little Feather, you know your pop is getting old. Excuse me now, for I'm going to turn in." Elijah went to Little Feather to embrace him again. "I'm so glad to see you. I love you as if you were my own son."

Little Feather replied, "I know. I know, and I love you too, Elijah." The girls looked on at the two men and so glad that their father was happy. The sisters held each other's hands in a silent agreement. Hilda looked at her sister, and then rose from her seat to leave.

"I'm coming Daddy," Hilda yelled behind her father as she went into the house. Susie was standing on the porch. Little Feather was stunned to see Susie had become just as beautiful as her mother, Snow Feather. Little Feather went to kiss Susie when she abruptly turned toward the moonlight. Little Feather attempted to kiss her again, but she stopped him directly with a soft but firm hand against his chest.

Little Feather stepped back, narrowing his eyes. "Don't tell me. It's that white man, isn't it?" Susie looked at Little Feather. She nodded yes.

The man was calm, but spoke matter-of-factly. "Susie, I know that I'm several years older than you. But I can give you peace, joy and understanding."

Susie interrupted his speech. "Little Feather, I really appreciate what you're trying to say to me. I love John. I've told Daddy, William, and now I'm telling you."

As Susie walked off the porch, Little Feather followed her. He grabbed her to turn her to face him. "I've always loved you Susie. I know it seems crazy to say now, but I could've had Matilda, but Matilda was too soft, just like your mother. I need a strong woman, Susie, like you, to make me feel loved and wanted."

"Little Feather, please stop," Susie said, but she turned to him and let him kiss her for the first time. For those ten seconds, Susie looked at Little Feather and thought, for a moment, that she wanted him, too. The kiss ended, and none too soon. By that time, William arrived at the house. Susie and Little Feather turned to greet William. William leapt from his buggy and ran to Little Feather.

They greeted each other like two children that loved each other for years. Susie looked at her brother and the man that was in love with her so happy with tears in her eyes. "Brother, it's good to see you once again." "How's Hilda?" William asked his sister.

"She's fine," Susie answered. "She's in the house getting Daddy ready for bed."

"Good!" William turned to Little Feather. "So how's Jacksonville?"

Little Feather answered gladly. "Everything is fine! Everybody has graduated from college and have gone on with their lives now." As they start to gather on the porch, Susie went into the house to get the men something to drink. Little Feather watched Susie go into the house, and then he grabs William by the arm. "Susie's really in love with John?" Little Feather sounded so disgusted.

"Well, it all started when you went away. John and I are best friends, but you know, Little Feather, I have always had the utmost respect for you. Elsie, John's sister, has been helping our people secretly with educational books for the children. The rest is history I must say." Little Feather nodded and shook his head so disappointedly. "Yeah, I figured something like that would happen when I went away."

"I heard that John is coming home soon," William said.

"Don't tell Susie yet, okay?" Little Feather said angrily. "I hope that I can change her mind."

"Good luck!" said William. "You know Susie has a strong mind."

Little Feather rose from the chair to say. "We'll see about that."

Susie came out to the porch with some herbal tea. "Little Feather, you're not leaving yet, are you? Please drink some tea with us."

Little Feather reluctantly answered. "No thanks, Susie. I must go see about my mother. I hope to see you tomorrow, though." He departed quickly.

Susie looked at William, puzzled. "What was that all about?"

William took the glass of tea to answer his sister. "You know what that was all about Susie. I saw Little Feather kissing you as I came up. It was none of my business, but Little Feather's been in love with you since the day you were born."

Susie dropped her head for a moment, then looked back up and stared into the trees in front of her. "William, what am I going to do?"

William touched his sister by the shoulder. "Susie, you've got to follow your heart. Otherwise, things can get pretty ugly."

Susie replied, "William, I know that my decision on this situation is going to be ugly. I just know that if I can get into the white man's world, I could do things for my people."

William looked at his sister and saw her resolve. "Sis, if that's the way you feel, then, I don't have anything to say about the matter."

Months passed. Little Feather stayed at the village and saw how rundown the settlement had become. Running Bear had gotten old, and Elijah's health was declining. The Indian village was going downhill. Some of the younger Indians moved away as the old Indians stayed to wilt and die. Hilda and Susie worked hard, trying to maintain the village as best they could.

John Quinton's return to town was without fanfare. In fact, he was there three months before

Susie and William learned that he was back in town. Little Feather found out, but he did not tell William. Little Feather knew what Elijah, his mentor, had taught him about the ways of the white man's world. What he learned helped him to stay on top of things. Ultimately, he knew that the world in which he lived, the white man would be on top.

One day, William went to see Elijah, furious at what he suspected, but he kept his composure until he saw his father Elijah. William showed up on his horse without his buggy. His sister watched him get off his horse. "Cheyenne! Stay, boy," he issued to his steed. William had kept that horse since Little Feather left him many moons ago. "Where's Father?"

Hilda pointed to where Elijah was as he was sitting down on the bank with some old Indian men from the village.

"Father, I must talk to you," William said sternly as he approached Elijah. As the old men stopped laughing about matters, Elijah looked at his son with a puzzled expression on his face. Elijah gets up from his seat to walk into the woods and listen to what his son has to say. "William, what is it that has you so upset?"

"I think Susie has run off to be with John so they can get married," William responded.

Chapter 10
Susie Marries John Quinton

"What?" It was as if the wind had been knocked out of the old man's gut. Elijah slumped down to the ground as the other Indian men tried to come to his help. "Oh, Great Spirit! Don't let my girl marry a white man." As the men carried Elijah to his house, Susie had run off to marry John Quinton. There was no one there from the tribe to witness the union, nor was there any one from his family. They got married in Orange County of Tallahassee.

Once they were married, John took a deep breath and said, "Susie, I love you, and I hope that my Mother will like you. She wanted me to marry that Brathwaithe girl, but I didn't like her. I love you, Susie. I know that our fathers haven't liked each other down through the years, but I can't see myself loving anyone else other than you."

John had his horse and buggy dressed in white linen, the fabric draped around the buggy, and Susie was dressed in a beautiful white lace Victorian gown with three-quarter sleeves which had beads hanging from them. Her feet were adorned with high-heeled ten-hole boots adorned with the Ivory beadwork. Susie was indeed something to behold on that day of September 17, 1912. Susie heard her father's voice and warnings in her head, but she knew without a shadow of doubt that she was supposed to marry John Quinton, son of the man that her father had hated for thirty years.

As John drove his bride to his house, Susie was in awe at the mansion that she envisioned in her mind; it made her think that this was where she belonged. The mansion was very elaborate. It had four columns at the front porch. The porch was covered with pink blossom flowers, and magnolias hung from the ceilings of the porch. The family was assemble themselves on the porch, waiting for John to bring home his bride. Mother Quinton stood up from her chair and saw that the woman that his son had married wasn't the one that she had selected for him. All of a sudden, Mother Quinton fainted. The black maids hurried to pick her up from the porch floor.

As Susie stepped out of the flower-covered buggy, disappointment filled her eyes. Elsie tried to feign surprise at not knowing who Susie was, as the bride ran up to her with a puzzled expression. She swallowed, with her big eyes streaming to look at Susie's gown, and said, "Hi, my name is Elsie. I'm pleased to meet you. Welcome to the Quinton house." John looked at his sister and rolled his eyes up in the air.

The maids gathered the couple's belongings and brought them into the house. Elton was in the den waiting on his son to come to him. "Where's Father?" John asked.

One of the maids told him, "Your father is waiting on you in the den, Mr. John." John took Susie by the arm to escort her into the house.

The foyer contained a Greek statue that had a fountain of streaming water; it stood in the center of the room. As she looked up the staircase, she saw a stained-glass window on the second–floor landing. The oak wood banister curved at each end, with giant pictures of their family hanging on the walls.

As John escorted Susie to see his father, she was trembling. Knowing what kind of man that he was, however, motivated her to keep her composure. "Hell, he tried to have sex with my sister," she thought to herself. The black maids opened the big doors to the den, and she noticed that the room was decorated with colors of wine and mint green. The wine leather sofa was huge with Victorian legs that curved to the floor. The imposing-looking draperies hanging from the window down to the floor were mint green with dark evergreen ties to hold them open. There were portraits of former mayors, judges, and a couple of presidents – Andrew Jackson and George Washington – that hung on the wall.

Elton was staring out the window, swirling some whiskey in the glass tumbler he held. He turned around and raised one eyebrow at Susie. He did not crack a smile. He moved his gaze to his son with disgust in his eyes. "So, this is your new squaw – I mean, bride."

John looked at his father and stilled the anger in his voice. "Yes, father, this is Susie Poohtawn, she's –"

"I know who she is." Elton moved his gaze once again to his son's new wife. "So, Susie? That's your name, isn't it?" Elton asked sternly.

"Yes, I'm Susie. Sir." Susie answered, never taking her eyes from his face. Susie tried very hard to not be disrespectful toward John's father.

Elton walked over to Susie as he put his glass down on the table. "You're welcome here as long as John loves you." The smile he gave her never reached his eyes. He cut his smile off to say, "In this house, the Quinton women have their place. Do you understand that, Miss Susie?" Elton looked at his son and waved them out of the room at the same time that the maids entered to announce, "Dinner is about to be served."

Mother Quinton collected herself enough to join the family for dinner. They all headed for the dining room, which was decorated with peach walls that held old pictures of their family above the buffet table. There was a giant grandfather clock placed in the corner. Susie was surprised when she noticed that they had an Indian statue placed by the door. The china on which dinner was served was elegant with green leaves and gold surrounding the plates.

Everyone sat down at the table, and Mother Quinton just stared at John with anger in her eyes. They said their Christian blessing over the meal, and Susie softly mumbled a native prayer to the Great Spirit. She would need divine assistance in this house. The maids came out with serving trays loaded with roasted duck, turkey, dressings, poke salad greens, macaroni and cheese and dinner rolls that were baked to a golden brown. Susie's mouth was watering, but she felt the unwelcoming eyes of her mother-in-law staring in her direction.

Elsie cleared her throat and began to speak, attempting to break the rime of ice that was forming at the table. "Well, it sure is a blessing to have another addition to the family."

A sound came from Elton, something midway between a grunt and a snort. As he continued to gobble his food up, the rest watched

Susie to see if she knew how to use the right eating utensils. The maids came out with peach cobbler. Once the meal was finished, Susie wiped her mouth with her napkin to say to her mother-in-law, "The dinner was delicious." Mother Quinton took a deep breath to address her daughter-in-law, but as the nasty retort rose in her throat, John cut his mother off to say, "Darling, I'm glad that you like this lovely dinner." Susie looked at John, recognizing what he had done, and slowly inhaled and exhaled to fix her breathing.

Mother Quinton turned to her son once again. "Isn't it about time you escort your wife to your bungalow?"

John answered hurriedly. "Yes mother. Susie?" Susie rose from her chair and reached for her husband's extended hand. Elsie was smiling happily. Mother Quinton looked at Elsie and batted her eyes in the air.

John took Susie up the stairs and then swept her off her feet as he carried her to his bedroom. He opened the door and saw that the maids had decorated the room with pale blue and green drapes with the bedspread to match. Victorian doors opened to a veranda at the front of the house, where the oak trees, so tall and strong, were swaying a breeze.

John picked his wife up once again to swing her around in the room. As he kisses his wife in the upstairs bedroom, a hard-driven horse pulled a buggy up to the front porch and came to a rapid stop. It was Elijah and William. They knocked on the door urgently. Elton and his wife were in the den talking about their son's decision for marriage.

The butler opened the door. Elijah comes in hurriedly, without giving the butler the chance to announce him. "I want to see my daughter!"

A startled Elton brought out a gun from under his coat. "Now wait a minute Elijah! You don't come into my house with that kind of attitude making any kind of demands."

Elijah was not listening to Elton. "Susie, Susie, get down here!" Elijah bellowed.

Susie heard the ruckus downstairs and looked at John. "Oh John, it's my father!"

John held Susie and told her, "Go downstairs and see your father. I'll be waiting for you." John stepped out onto the upstairs terrace to hear the conversation.

Susie walked downstairs to greet her brother and her father. She walks slowly toward them, as if she had done nothing wrong. "Father, what is the matter with you?"

"I want you to come home, Susie," Elijah said as he grabbed his daughter by the arm. Susie snatched herself away from her father for the first time ever in her life, while William looked at this sister with disgust.

Susie leveled her gaze at her Elijah. "Father, I'm married now. I knew that you would disapprove. That's why I ran off with John."

`"But Susie, Little Feather came home for YOU!" Elijah said with conviction in his voice

Susie turned away. "Father, what could Little Feather offer me? I know Little Feather loves me, but I love John." John was listening upstairs, shaking his head with agreement. William turned then to look up at the veranda. John saw this in time to turn back into the bedroom.

Elijah sighs to say. "Remember what I've told you. If you find a way to come home, you are welcome. I know that you will come home, but in the meantime, be watchful for you will see of which I speak. I love you my daughter. Take care of yourself." He hugs his daughter and William followed suit.

Elijah turns to look at Elton, "You'd better not hurt my daughter, or I'll come after you, Elton Quinton."

Elton just looked at Elijah. As Elijah and William ran off quickly in their horse and buggy, Susie ran past her in-laws to run upstairs to John. She jumped in John's arms and just cried. John just held his wife to let her get it all out. He picked her up and laid her on the bed to kiss her and embrace her.

John got up to take his shirt off. He hurried to lift Susie up to take off her dress as well. The night breeze in the air was making trees move swiftly and the wind made the leaves create a whistling sound in the air. As the couple looked at each other, with fiery passion flowing in their veins, they both laid down to make love on a September night.

The morning came. Susie awoke to discover that her husband was not there with her. The maids came in the room to prepare her for breakfast. They opened up the Victorian doors for the air to come in. "Where's my husband?" Susie asked

One of the maids replied, "Miss Susie, don't worry. Mr. John had some business to take care of. He'll be back." Susie looked so disappointed. She took a deep breath as the maids opened her boudoir to select something for her to wear. Susie looks at the African women with admiration; their careful attention gave her so much comfort.

Susie puts on a mint green dress, white lace trimming her sleeves and the hem of her dress. They leave her, and she walked downstairs to meet everybody. She heard some voices in the den. It was Elton and his men talking. She went to the door and heard one of the men say, "Well, Elton, how do you like your squaw daughter-in-law?" One of them started laughing.

Elton answered angrily. "I don't think a damned thing is funny. Hell, I told my son not to marry those damned Indian women in the first place."

Susie gasped, and then looked around to see if someone had seen her. She hurriedly ran into the kitchen to see Mother Quinton and Elsie prepare for breakfast. As they turned to see her approach the kitchen door, Susie composed herself enough to extend a greeting, "Good morning, everybody."

Mother Quinton said coolly, "Good Morning Susie. Glad that you could join us. Come outside onto the terrace." Susie followed them as she stepped out to the back of the house. She saw a huge expanse of land that stretched out from the back yard for as far as the eye could see. Watching the field hands harvesting the crops for the winter, she thought about her people. Mother

Quinton interrupts her thoughts to ask her, "Are you all right?"

Susie turned and sat down at the table to be served breakfast. "Yes, Mother Quinton, I'm alright. Why do you ask?"

Mother Quinton answered, "After that commotion last night, I didn't think things was going to be right between you and John."

Susie smiled thinking about their honeymoon night in her in-laws' home. "I'm just fine. When is John coming home?"

Mother Quinton smiled and answered, "Child, John is a very busy man. He'll be here for lunch."

Susie continued to look out at the land that the Quintons possessed. The summer breeze kissed her face, and it was if she heard her father speaking to her once again.

As they finished breakfast, Mother Quinton got up from the table and said, "Susie, I know this is very new to you. We, the Quinton women, do stay in our place. If there ever comes a time that you can't handle that, we would surely know how to deal with it."

Elsie interrupted to say. "Mother, have you heard from Jenny?" Mother Quinton looked at Elsie with a surprised look on her face, as if to shun what Elsie had mentioned.

Chapter 11
Susie Finds a Secret

Susie waited to hear what was going to be said. Mother Quinton told Susie, "Child, why don't you go to the front porch. We'll be out there in a minute."

Mother Quinton grabbed Elsie by the arm to take her into the hallway from the kitchen. "Don't you dare bring up family matters in front of that Indian, Elsie," Mother Quinton said crossly. "Something tells me that you've been running your mouth again."

Elsie snatched her arm away from her mother. "I haven't said anything. How do you know that John hasn't told Susie about OUR family issues?" Elsie said with contempt.

"Jenny has been gone out of our lives for ten years, and we're intending to keep it that way. Do you understand that, Elsie?" Mother Quinton's eyes were stern.

"Yes, mother, I understand," Elsie turned to go rejoin Susie out on the porch. Elsie took a deep breath, as she waves her brown long hair away from her face. "So, Susie, are you all right?" Elsie asks.

Susie answered, "Yes, I'm fine. I'm just waiting for John." Her curiosity got the best of her as she revisited the subject at hand. "Elsie, what's going on with Mother Quinton not answering you about Jenny?"

Elsie shushed Susie with her fingers. "It seems that we're not ever going to see Jenny again. I really miss my sister, Susie. One day I'm going to find out where she is and I'm going to take her out of that asylum that mom and dad put her in." Elsie didn't know that Mother Quinton was listening to her divulge their family secrets from the hallway. She threw up her hands and turned toward the den get a drink.

All of a sudden, John came up the road with his horses. Susie stood up to see her husband arrive. She left the porch to greet him. John looked upset as he remembered his confrontation with William in town. "How could you snatch my sister away from her father in his old days?" His childhood friend asked him.

John tried to keep these thoughts from showing on his face. He got out of the horse and buggy to embrace his wife. Should he tell her? "Hello, Darling. I'm sorry that I had to leave out so early this morning. I had some things to do."

"That's all right. As long you don't make it a habit." Susie smiles at her husband as they walked up to the porch. Elsie was standing there watching them in awe. "Hi, Sis." John kissed his sister on the cheek. "How's mother?"

Elsie takes a deep breath. "Oh, she's in the parlor."

John says. "Honey, meet me in the bedroom, won't you?"

Susie told Elsie, "I'll see you later, Elsie." Susie smiled as she went upstairs.

John walked into the den to find his mother alone in the room, drinking, and seemingly enjoying herself, "Mother, what are you doing?" Mother Quinton was lying on the couch, drunk. Mother Quinton opens her eyes as they rolled back in her head.

"Son, you're home." She started to lift herself up. "I thought I would come in here to think about Jenny." Mother Quinton started to cry. "I can't stand this! But there's nothing that I can do about it."

John took his mother by the shoulders, "Yes there is, Mother. The only thing you need to do is to tell me where she is."

"Elton will kill me if I told you all," the old woman said despairingly. John took his mother into his arms and held her as she cried on John's shoulder.

One of the maids came into the room and asked, "Is there anything I can do, Mr. John?" John nodded with his head for the maid to take Mother Quinton to her bedroom. Mother Quinton was still sobbing. Susie was patiently waiting for John to come into their bedroom. Susie had changed into a beautiful white gown with lace around her shoulders and sleeves.

John walks in to see his beautiful wife lying on their sofa. He walks toward her and held her tightly. Susie asked him, "Is everything all right honey?"

John stood up to take off his coat and take off his tie and placed it on the chair. "I don't know, Susie. I thought when we got married that everything would be all right, but now I am not so sure. I saw William in town today, and he's very angry with me." Susie got up from the sofa looking concerned.

"I'm sorry that I left Hilda there with Daddy. "Perhaps this Saturday I could go see them. Would that be okay with you?" Susie asked.

John answered, "Sure, go see them. In the meantime, I want to love you and love you." He picked Susie up and kissed her tenderly. John continued to kiss her as he placed Susie on the bed. The wind was blowing into the room as John made love to his wife. His whispering to her became a mantra, "I love you, Susie. I love you."

Susie's Hearing Secrets

The evening came. Elton and his men had convened once again in the den discussing political issues. John was in there with them. The men were drinking, laughing and talking when suddenly one of the men asked, "Elton, what are we going to do with them damned Indians and them niggers that are living on the east side of town?" John stopped lowered his drink from his lips and looked at his father.

Elton asked the man, "What do you mean? Let me tell you something. For twenty years, I have been dealing with them. You know what my daddy would say. 'Leave them alone. They will destroy themselves. Just keep them in their place.'"

John looked up at the ceiling. "What is that to you, Mr. Johnson? You don't say that when you've been going to those parlors getting some sex from those women as you call them."

Elton shouted to John. "John! Watch your mouth!"

"Can't we talk about other issues besides trying to destroy someone's life? Those people have had enough of you all destroying their lives!" John put his drink down and left out of the den. Having to backtrack her steps, Susie almost was caught as she pretended to come down the stairs for the first time.

John saw Susie's second descent from the stairs. "Darling, are you ready to eat dinner?"

Susie sighed and said, "Yes, let's go eat." Susie placed Mr. Johnson in her mind so that she would not forget what he said. Susie realizes now that she's got to keep her ears and eyes open in case the white man start some commotion with her people. She looked up to see Mother Quinton coming down for dinner; Susie thought that she looked like a train had ran over her. The maids had done their best to make her look presentable.

Elton came in to join them as he lets his men out the door. Susie felt such contempt for her father-in-law; she wanted to beat the shit out of him. She managed to hold her composure and smile at her husband. Everybody was quite solemn when they ate dinner. Elton wiped his mouth from eating some chicken and dumplings and finally broke the silence at the table. "So, son, how's business?"

John looked up at his father. "Quite well, Dad. I have to cover some land business with Mr. McElroy."

Elton pretended he was trying to remember the name. "McElroy, McElroy. Oh, yes, that Irishman that moved here from the west."

John went on to say, "Well, it seems that the land he owns belongs to that black man named Jefferson. Jefferson wants to deal with him but he's making sure that he's going to keep half of his land."

Elton asked, "Well, what's the problem?"

"Well, Mr. McElroy found out that Jefferson is black, and he doesn't want to deal with him."

Mother Quinton jumped in to contribute to the conversation with a derisive snort. "That's absurd. I'm so sick of this prejudiced stuff that I don't know what to do."

Elton replied, "Oh darling, that's just business. It is why a woman does not have any business knowing about business. Y'all put your feelings into it way too much. Son, I'll see what I can do. How much is this land worth?"

"Ten-thousand dollars," John answered.

Water spurted from Elton's mouth in surprise, and he started to cough from choking. He cleared his throat and wiped his mouth and chin. Mother Quinton raised her eyebrows up as she ended her laughter. "I bet you that would change your mind, now wouldn't it, Elton? When it comes to money, you'll do anything." Her laughter was gone completely as she glared in her husband's face and walked out of the dining room. Elsie and Susie just sat there in silence, taking it all in.

Susie stood up from the table suddenly. "Someone go after Mother Quinton because I have an announcement." John looked surprised to hear what Susie had to say.

Elsie said, "I'll go get her."

As Elsie went to get Mother Quinton, Elton put his hand over his forehead and sighed about coming news. Mother Quinton reentered the dining room. Mother Quinton was looking at Elton with disgust; she rolled her eyes at him as he tried to take her by the hand. Mother Quinton snatched her hand away from him. Susie thought about Hilda at the parlor, about to service men like Elton Quinton.

"Everyone!" Susie took John's hand as she looked around the table. "We are proud to announce that we're expecting a baby this fall."

Mother Quinton fainted again. Elton, not sure how to feel about this news, got up from his chair to greet his son. While Elsie grabbed Susie so thrilled at this bit of information, Susie realized that Mother Quinton had fainted – again. Susie smiled and held John tightly.

As the dusk fell, John and Susie were swinging on the swing on the porch enjoying the night. John tells his wife, "Susie, I don't want you to ever feel that your husband is out here doing some bad business deals. Look at me! Yeah, I know that there is a lot of crooked-handed stuff is going around. I'm not going to ever let this interfere with our lives. Yes, I will try to see if your people will be all right, too. I cannot say anything for the black people. They are not my concern."

Susie answered to say, "When it comes to those black men coming up dead for no reason, you got to find a way to make sure that their issues don't become ours. I mean it, John," she continued as she got up from between his legs. "The moment I find out that you have your hand in that stuff, I will leave for good." John held onto Susie for another moment; he realized that he had married a smart woman who was aware of what was happening around her. She knew that some bad things were going on. Susie gently broke away from John's hold to tell him, "I'm going to bed." She leaves John on the porch. Elton quietly moved by Susie, passing her in the hallway as he went onto the porch with John.

Elton looked back inside the house where is daughter-in-law had just stood, and then looked at his son. He sat down in the chair, noticing at the fireflies flying around the front yard like lightning streaking through the trees. "You know son, ever since I was born, I never could understand what could be so wrong between different races of men. Some time ago, when I was a child, I, too, thought that I could be friends with that Indian named White Cloud. My daddy would not allow me to play with him. I see that history repeats itself over and over again. No matter what you do or don't do in your life, life will play tricks on you to make you be the man that you're supposed to be.

"I knew that Susie's father and I wouldn't get along. It's just the way life is. I must see to it that those niggers and those Indians do not get ahead of us.

"If I had spent more time with you kids, maybe things wouldn't be the way they are now, but that's the past. What Jenny did was a disgrace to this family. She'll never come this way again."

John looked at his father. "Dad, you're wrong. When it comes to love between two people, there is nothing you can do about it. Jenny loved Buddy, and you took that away from her by killing that man."

Elton wiped his hands to put his hands to his forehead. "I did it. Yes, I did it. To say that I regret it, yes, I do. I should not have killed him. He was one of my best hands. I have not had a good hand since. Perhaps I never will and that may be my punishment. John, when it comes time that this place won't be anymore, burn this sucker down, because I'll be damned if a nigger lives in this house." Elton turned his face from the land to look at his son. "Will you promise me that?"

John shook his head in disgust. "You know what? That's why things ain't never going to be right with people like you around." John left his father to go upstairs to see that his wife was sound asleep. John started to wake her, but he just sat in the chair and fell asleep with the words that he heard come out of his father's mouth.

The morning came. John was gone again. The maids were helping Susie with her morning sickness. Elsie came in to see about Susie and the maids left. Elsie walked over to the bed to console Susie. Susie said with a hoarse voice, "Oh Elsie, this is killing me." Susie tries to get up when Elsie stops her. Elsie props Susie's pillows up to help her to feel more comfortable. "Elsie, I heard your father and John talking last night. It was ugly. I'm going to go see my father on Saturday. I miss my people very much. Don't you worry about me. I hate to say this, but your father has a lot to answer for when he dies."

Elsie asked, "What are you talking about?"

Susie took Elsie by the hand. "If there comes a time when I have to leave this house, I'm going to find out where Jenny is. And you're going to help me." Elsie hugged Susie. Elsie had started to cry when Mother Quinton came into the bedroom.

"Well, well, well. I see that my girls are up here having a chat. So, what are you two up to? Susie, do you need some crackers? How about some of your Indian tea?" Susie and Elsie just looked at Mother Quinton as if someone had hit her on her head with a bag of compassion.

The older woman answered the disbelief on their faces. "I'm so excited that we're going to have a new one in this family. There haven't been a baby since Jen– I mean, oh well, it's been twenty-five years."

The younger women saw that Mother Quinton had a little drink on her breath. Elsie walked over to her mother. "Mother, are you all right?"

Mother Quinton moved away from her daughter to walk toward Susie. "Now, darling, everything's going to be all right."

Susie raised her eyebrows in suspicion at Mother Quinton. "I hear that you're going to see your father. I'd never seen him until he came here on your wedding day. My, my, my. He was a handsome man at one time, or so I've heard throughout the years."

Susie asks her mother-in-law, "Mother Quinton, what are you talking about?"

"Well, child, when you go see your father, tell him that Mother Quinton asked about him, okay?"

Elsie was embarrassed as she looked at her mother. "Mother, don't you have something else to do?" Elsie turns to Susie so that her mother can leave.

"Okay, I'm leaving. Susie, don't forget." Mother Quinton smiled mysteriously and winked. Susie says. "What was that all about?"

Elsie answered, "I don't know, but I do know one thing. I'm going to find out. But then again, I'm going to wait to see what comes out of this." They start laughing together.

Susie asks Elsie, "Are you still visiting my village to see how the children are doing?

"Not lately, but there is this Indian there that looks so sad," Elsie replied.

Susie's eyes got big. "Oh really? What does he look like?"

"Well, he's handsome and tall. He hangs around your father." Susie knew that she was describing Little Feather. She thought the last time she was with him when he came back from Jacksonville. A tear came out of her eye and she wiped her cheek to keep Elsie from seeing it. She did not move quickly enough. "What's wrong with you?" Elsie looked surprised.

"It's nothing Elsie. I'll be glad to see my people."

"Want me to go with you?" Elsie asked.

"No!" Susie said quickly. "I'll be fine."

Saturday morning came. John was there that morning. As he helped his wife prepare for the trip, John kept looking at Susie as if she missed something or someone. Susie looked at John. "What is the matter with you? You look kind of lonesome." Susie smiles because she knows what John is thinking.

John answers and shrugs it off. "Oh, nothing. Will you be home by sunset?"

"John, I need to see my daddy before the fall comes. What are you worried about? I'm having your baby shouldn't that be enough for you?"

John smiles, and grins, saying, "I don't mean any harm. Susie, be careful, okay?"

As the driver takes Susie on her journey, everybody on the porch watched her leave. Susie giggled at the knowledge that she has made an impression on the family, when at first they didn't like her. Since learning that Mother Quinton became an alcoholic because her husband sent her daughter away, because she became pregnant by a black man, Susie's entire outlook on the family seemed much bleaker than she first thought.

She sighs as she thought about Little Feather; maybe, just maybe it wouldn't have been such a bad thing after all to have married him. After all, John disappears in the morning without waking her up. Something was going on. Susie took a deep breath and thought, "What goes on in the dark must come to the light."

Chapter 12
Susie Visits Family

Susie was coming over to the ridge. The old Indian women were in their yards planting flowers. The Indian children were playing marbles, and playing tag. The old men were gathered together in a circle. Their houses were in serious disrepair and their roofs needed a lot work done on them.

One of the Indian children yelled, "It's Susie!"

The coach approached the center of the village to get to her Daddy's house. The Indians waved. Susie waved back at them, glad to see everybody. Elijah and Hilda were sitting on the porch. Hilda got off the porch to greet her sister. "Susie, thank God!" Hilda couldn't wait for her sister to get out of the coach. "I'm so glad to see you," Hilda said as she started to cry.

Susie held her sister and waited for her to stop crying. They looked at each other, and Hilda wiped her eyes on her apron. Elijah was sitting in his favorite chair on the porch. He was smoking his pipe, his tall black hat was on his head and he didn't say a word. Hilda looked at Susie with surprise as she discovered that her sister was expecting. Hilda grabbed her sister again.

"Hi Daddy! How are you?" Susie greeted her father. As Susie walked toward her father, he looked past her into the sky.

He said, "You'd better hope that baby got some of me in him." Hilda and Susie started laughing.

Susie kissed her father on his face. "Daddy, I've felt you so much, and I knew that I had to come to see about you."

Elijah said, "Little Feather's been awfully sad since you left here, Susie. You broke his heart."

Susie puts her head in her Daddy's lap to say. "I know Daddy."

Elijah explained. "If you had a waited, Little Feather would've made you very happy."

Hilda interrupted to say, "Susie, come inside. I've got something to show you." Susie stepped inside the house. Hilda had painted the big room with almond and green. She walked over to the kitchen where Daddy had made some cabinets to make the kitchen have space.

Hilda handed Susie a beautiful brown, almond, and green crocheted blanket for the baby. Susie, in turn, pulled out a present for Hilda. It was some good smelling salts, and candles that smelled like lavender. They embraced each other warmly.

Susie gave Hilda some tobacco for their father. Susie said, "Hilda, the house looks nice!"

Hilda smiled and said, "After you left, I spent my time fixing up the house." Susie looked at Hilda as if Hilda knew what her sister was wondering.

"Little Feather knows you're here. I don't think that he wants to see you like this." Hilda finished by asking her sister, "Are you really happy with those white folks?"

Susie sat Hilda down to tell her everything about the Quintons. While they were laughing and giggling, Little Feather stepped in the door. Susie and Hilda stopped laughing. Susie looked at Little Feather with astonishment. "Little Feather! I'm so glad to see you." She went to embrace him as Hilda quietly went outside. Little Feather embraced Susie as if he did not want to let her go. "Susie, you look so beautiful. Is this how pregnant women look?"

Susie grinned at her old friend. "Oh Little Feather, you're just teasing me. Sit down. I have something to tell you." Little Feather sat down, never moving his gaze from Susie.

"Little Feather, I'm sorry that I hurt you." Little Feather started to say something, but Susie would not let him. "The way I feel right now, I have thoughts of you. I feel you in the breeze in the day as well as the night. I know that's wrong because I'm married."

"As long as I keep you in my thoughts and my heart, you will always be here with me in spirit." Little Feather gets up to turn away toward the window. "I knew I shouldn't have come here, but I wanted to see you too, Susie. I will always love you. If you ever need me, you let me know okay?" He turns and starts to kiss Susie on her head, but he stopped and embraced her completely.

Hilda came back into the room. "Are you two staying for dinner?"

Little Feather said, "Very funny, Hilda." Hilda smiled.

Susie said, "I'm staying for dinner, but I must get back home before it gets dark."

Hilda said, "Alright, then."

Elijah came inside to sit by the fireplace. A picture of their mother was on the mantle. Susie walked over to look at her mother. Hilda was almost finished cooking some roast deer and vegetables. Elijah looked at Susie and said, "Baby, everything is going to be all right. I see everything has come to a head, hasn't it? I told you it would. Don't you trust those white folks, for they are the blue-eyed devils on this earth!"

Susie remembered her mother-in-law and turned to her father. "Daddy, Mother Quinton says hello."

"Who?" Elijah asked puzzled. "Aww, your crazy mother-in-law?" Elijah started to laugh. "I remember in my younger days, Miss Eleanor – that's her name – tried to make advances."

Hilda raised her head from the cooking pot. "Daddy!" Susie started laughing.

"I ain't lying!"" the Indian chief retorted. "She was pretty, too. But she's crazy."

Susie told Elijah. "Daddy, she drinks like a fish."

"Hell, she always has and that's why I didn't get involved with her. I knew no one could touch my Snow Feather. She was the most beautiful woman in this region, and better looking than those rich, ugly white women in town." Susie and Hilda just smiled proudly.

As the Poohtawn family ate their dinner with much happiness in their hearts, Hilda almost started to cry again, remembering that Susie had to go back to town. "How's William?" Elijah answered. "I haven't seen William. Hilda, have you seen William?"

Hilda choked back tears to answer her father. "No Daddy."

"Since you got married Susie, no one has seen him. He told me that he had a confrontation with your husband."

Susie looked surprised and asked, "When?"

Elijah said proudly. "Oh, way back as you were in wedded bliss."

Hilda looked at Susie and turned her head. Susie threw her napkin down angrily at the secret. Elijah exclaimed. "Aww, Susie, they'll be okay. Since you've been pregnant, I guess you don't go into town. That is what those men do to their women. Keep them barefoot and pregnant."

"Daddy, could you get the coach ready for me? Hilda, I'm sorry that I have to go. I will let you know when I have the baby so you can come to see me. I'll send for you." She gave her sister a kiss on the cheek. Elijah got up from the table and continued to laugh as he went into his bedroom. Susie got into the coach. Little Feather watched Susie leave and they waved goodbye at each other.

Susie started to cry after learning that her brother was going to stop her from marrying John.

John was in a hurry to get married. Susie knew then what she had to do. She couldn't keep getting pregnant by John. Otherwise, she would be done for, for the rest of her life. She remembered something that her Daddy told her long ago. "Don't ever kiss no one's ass." William was coming to her mind. "You and Hilda will always be together." What did all of this mean?

As Susie approached town, she was on her way to the mansion, but as she turned her head away from the window, she saw William going into the Parlor. Susie yelled out of the window. "William! William!"

William turned to see his sister. Susie told the coachman to stop the carriage as William ran up to the coach. "Susie, what are you doing here in town?"

"William, we need to talk," Susie tells her brother. "And it's not about Daddy!"

Susie continues angrily, "William, why didn't you tell me that Little Feather wanted to marry me but instead allowed John to beat him to the punch?"

William explained. "Susie, I really didn't want you to marry either of them at that time! I just happened to tell John that Little Feather was in town to stay. I didn't think anything was going to come out of it. I see now that that was not the case. Yes, I'm mad at John, but I've got to get over it." William then looks at his sister with narrowed eyes. "Sis, are you pregnant?"

"Yes William, and don't change the subject _"

William hollered out. "Ah-ha! Hey! I'm going to be an Uncle."

Susie started smiling. "William, we've got to keep in contact with each other. I've got a feeling that something bad is going to happen."

William's eyes narrow again. "What's the matter with you?"

"John's supposed to be selling some land to this Irishman named McElroy, but he doesn't want to buy from a black man named Jefferson."

"So, what's that got to do with us?" William asked.

Susie answered, "You don't get it, do you? They might do something to Jefferson so that he won't get any profit off his own land!"

William stared hard and long at his sister. "Sis, don't you worry about this matter. I will see what I can do, okay? Susie, whatever you do, you've got to stay calm. Remember, you live with those people. Elton F. Quinton is nobody to play with, Susie. Stay out of his way. Do you hear me?"

As the sun was going down on the Quinton estate, the Quintons were anxiously waiting for

Susie. "It's getting late John. Your wife shouldn't be out there by herself." Mother Quinton was getting nervous.

Elsie said, "Don't worry about Susie. She is a strong woman. That's something that we ought to give her credit for."

Chapter 13
Susie Confronts John

Susie was came up into the roadway. Everybody stood up from the porch. "I hear horses! It's Susie!" Elsie said loudly.

John walked down the roadway to greet his wife. The coachman came up toward the house as John opens the door of the carriage to lift his wife out of the carriage. Susie says under her breath. "I need to talk to you, John Quinton." John looks at Susie in confusion. He faked a smile on his face as Elsie comes to greet Susie. "Susie, how was your trip? We were worried about you."

"Worried about me? You need to worry about your brother." Susie accepted Elsie's embrace. The black maids came out to accommodate Susie. "John, I need to see you right now!" Mother Quinton looked toward the porch to see that Susie is very angry. As John follows Susie upstairs, Mother Quinton said. "I guess I'll go into the den and fix me a drink." Elsie just stood there on the porch not knowing what to do.

As John opens the bedroom door while Susie walks past him without any embrace. The bedroom door was barely closed again before she rounded on her husband. "Why didn't you tell me that you talked to William before we got married?"

"What do you mean Susie? I thought that you loved me!" John had a sinking feeling of where this was going.

"I do, John – I do. But it wasn't fair to me even though you knew that Little Feather loved me, too."

John stood there, dumbstruck. Not knowing what to say, he opened his arms and said, "Susie, I love you, and I'm so sorry. I thought that you wanted to get out of –"

Susie interrupted him. "Get out of what, John Quinton? The Indian village?

"Let me tell you something, John. I'm proud of who I am and where I came from. Did you think that bringing me here to this insane asylum was going to make me forget my people?" Elsie and Mother Quinton were listening in the hallway. When Susie's statement rose on a shriek for them to hear, Mother Quinton choked on her drink. "I can't listen to this anymore."

Elsie whispered, "Wait a minute, Mama. It's getting better."

John was pleading with his wife. "Susie, Susie, Susie! Please, you're pregnant." Elsie laughed because John didn't know what to say.

"Don't 'Susie' me! You think your Daddy and Mama's scaring me about me being 'in my place' in this house? You wait until I have this baby. Uh-huh. That's alright, John. You'll soon see what I'm saying."

John sighed and walked over to his wife. "Baby, now that you've said your peace, I just want to say, still, I love you."

Susie looked at her husband and shook her head at him. Then they both started to laugh together. Mother Quinton and Elsie were still listening as they put their hands together. Mother Quinton said, "I surely misunderstood her. I can rest now, 'cause Susie's got spunk." Elsie laughed at her mother as they walk away from the door.

Autumn came. The Cherokee were having their festival. Susie was huge. Elsie was aware of what was going on. Elsie planned on going, and Susie was getting very uneasy because she wanted to go. While Elsie was in her sister-in-law's room, trying to help her, Elsie said, "Don't worry Susie. I will make sure that Hilda will be here when you have the baby, okay?" Susie wondered to herself, not so certain that would be the case.

People in town attended the Indian Festival. The event happened in September as the leaves turns red, gold, and brown. The African women on the plantation often wondered about the festival that they used to have. Some of the women kept Susie company since John was not coming home until late at night. While Elsie was gone, Susie called for some of the black maids to assist her in her bath.

As Susie glanced at the two women, she wondered about them. What made the white man bring these people to serve them? Why would she want these women to serve her? In her village, the older women serve the family for special occasions. For other white people to serve each other, that wasn't happening. Hell, as far as Susie could see, she wouldn't want a white woman serving her for any reason.

As the black women was getting her out of the tub, she told one of them to fetch her some of her Indian tea that she brought back from home. She decided to ask a question to one of the black women. "Do you like it here in this land?"

The African woman looked at Susie with surprise. "I'm not allowed to talk to you. I'm only supposed to serve you, ma'am."

"Um-hum," Susie responded. "Well, let me say this. For years, both your people and my people have been at a disadvantage because of the white man. By me being Cherokee, my ways are going to help me to get to where I'm going. Confidentially speaking, I know that I'm not going to be here very long. I suggest that y'all do the same."

After that talk, the other African woman came to clean up for Susie. As Susie put on her gown, she grabbed the African woman and offered, "If you want to come with me that day, you're welcome to do so." The African woman looked, smiled and nodded shortly at Susie to accept her offer. Susie then went out onto the terrace to feel the breeze when suddenly fireworks were in the air to the east of her location. She smile happily in that direction because she knew that her people were having a good time.

John came into the bedroom. He watched Susie out on the terrace and knew she was thinking of her people and their celebration. He took off his coat, tie and laid them on the back of the chair. He laid his hands on her shoulders and dropped a kiss on one of them.

"Hello, darling." John stood behind his wife holding her.

"Isn't it beautiful John? The Great Spirit in the Sky is happy that my people are celebrating their harvest."

"Oh yeah?" John answered.

"Yeah, what do your people do?" Susie turns around in front of John.

"My people celebrate in the early spring. We did not go this year but next year I will make sure that we go. We allow your people come to sell their goods, too."

Susie was excited, "Oh yeah?"

John took his wife by the arms and said, "Oh yeah!" Susie started laughing as she looks at her husband to see love in his eyes. The family had not come back yet. John pulled Susie back into the bedroom to lay her down on the bed. As John was getting excited, Susie stopped him. John looked at Susie puzzled. "What's the matter?"

Susie asked, "Do you want this baby to come fast?"

John was frustrated, "Baby, I want you." As Susie looked out of the window to see the fireworks, she thought about Little Feather and knew that he was making them happen.

Susie allowed her husband to make love to her so that he could go to sleep. The family returned to the house. Susie snuck to the door to meet Elsie when she heard Mother Quinton say, "It's a damn shame that Elijah didn't recognize me." Susie laughs under her breath.

She heard Elsie say, "I had a good time with our Cherokee neighbors." Elsie didn't tell anyone that she herself had been cavorting with an Indian. Susie didn't even know. It seemed that the white men in town did not want to cavort with Elsie because she was barren.

Mother Quinton kissed her daughter goodnight. As Elsie went into her room, Susie knocked on the door. Elsie opened the door gladly. She pulled Susie into the room. "Susie, you missed everything! I had a wonderful time!" Elsie threw herself on her bed.

Elsie's room was beautiful with peach and green with a little white Victorian picture frames and statues on her wall. Her room faced the back of the house showing acres of land. Susie hit Elsie on the arm from curiosity. "Well, what happened? Did you see Hilda and Little Feather? Elsie, who were you with there?"

"Susie, there's this Indian named - what his name?" Elsie was so giddy and confused. "Aww, his name is Big Cloud." Susie's mouth dropped wide open, because she knew that he's Running Bear's oldest son.

Susie started to laugh out loud.

Elsie said, "Shhh! Be quiet before Mother hears us."

Susie couldn't stop laughing. "Big Cloud is so crooked and huge that the other Indian women have nothing to do with him." Susie couldn't get it out of her mouth to say as she laughed so hard. She looked at Elsie, shaking her head holding her mouth with her hands to shut herself up. Finally she asked, "Elsie, how did you handle Big Cloud? Girl, don't you know he's huge?"

Elsie looked at her sister-in-law as she crosses her arms to her breast. Elsie said, "I don't care. I had a great moment in my life. He didn't hurt me because he did something for me that I didn't know existed."

Susie laughed again. "Big Cloud wanted Hilda, but she cursed at him. I ain't never going to forget that." Susie chuckled and continued to say, "Well, sister-in-law, I'm glad that you had a good time."

"Little Feather said that he was going to light the fireworks for you because you liked them," Elsie said.

Susie looked at Elsie, "Yeah, I guess you've heard the story."

Elsie walks over to her sister-in-law and sighed, "You're a lucky woman, Susie. You have two men that love you. I've just got to get it when it comes."

Susie hugged Elsie and said, "You be careful though, because some men out there ain't no good."

"I know," Elsie replied. "I've already called your brother out. See you in the morning."

Chapter 14
Susie Has a Baby

The month of September passed away as Susie gave birth to Elijah Fitzgerald Quinton. He was a beautiful baby boy. He had brown, curly locks on his head. His skin was red just like her daddy. His ears were big like her daddy. His eyes were hazel, though, and he weighed eight pounds. The baby's hands were large just like his feet. As everybody was in the bedroom looking at the couple admiring the baby, Elsie went out into the hallway to cry.

Mother Quinton looked at the baby and then left. She was upset that the baby really didn't look like them. Elton was angry because Susie named the baby after his daddy. He got up to leave. The doctor left, too. John was mesmerized by his son. He didn't care who he looked like. He knew that the boy was his son. John climbed into bed with his wife. After what the Doctor had told him what he could and couldn't do, John held his son up in the air.

"This is my son. Susie, isn't he strong?"

Susie looked at the both of them. "John, this is your son. In whom my Great Spirit is well pleased."

The African women came to assist them with their baby. As the African maids took the baby out of John's arms, the African woman looked at the baby and noticed that the Indian blood flowed in the baby's veins. The African woman smiled as she placed the baby in a beautiful cradle trimmed in gold and white, and covered with a white sheer veil.

It was November twenty-six, in the year 1915. A lot of things were going on at that time. The Ku Klux Klan was killing black men one after another. Woodrow Wilson was President at the time. He allowed many things to happen to

Indians and Black folk. The winter had come. Christmas was coming. The Quintons had their house decorated with beautiful white lights hanging from their porch.

While the Indians had their popcorn with so much colorful lights to shine on their houses, William and Elsie helped them to get Christmas lights. The baby was just two months old. Neither Hilda nor her brother William had come to see her nephew. Susie was a bit depressed. The winter had brought about some changes. In Florida, there was not any snow, but only cold breezes blew through the trees and weighed them down heavily.

Susie was trying to recover from giving birth. She had one more month until she turned eighteen. Susie was looking well and strong. John still was not coming home as he should. Susie continued to make the best out of things. She continued to talk to the African women about matters of their homeland. Some of them could not answer her, and their puzzled expressions showed their confusion at the news she shared with them.

Eleanor Quinton had grown closer to Susie. She did not think that she would ever be able to relate to her. Eleanor did not have too many friends. She and Elton would attend banquets and dinners together in public. Eleanor was always well dressed. Because of her drinking problem, Elton would leave her home because she could become quite embarrassing. Everybody in town had heard about what Elton had done to Jenny.

The other white women in the high society groups carried on with their lives, and would often exclude Mother Quinton from their activities. Lonely, she would get drunk in her own house. Susie started to realize that her mother-in-law needed comfort and love. Since the baby came into the house, Eleanor would come into their bedroom simply to look at him and leave. Elton would go to see the baby only if he was downstairs. Elton never went upstairs to John and Susie's bedroom.

It was Christmas, Susie's birthday. As Susie gets up, she sees that John was there for her. She was dressed in a beautiful red dress trimmed with white fringe on her sleeves and white fringe at the hem. Susie still had not heard from her people. As she pushed down her feelings, she noticed that she and her son were being taken care of. Susie was going to make sure that her mother in law would not spoil her day.

Elsie entered the bedroom and crowed, "Happy Birthday Susie! My, my, my, you're a spoiled woman to be born on Christmas Day!"

Susie signed and said, "It's not easy as it seems Elsie."

Elsie was confused. "What do you mean now, Susie? Are you talking about Hilda and

William not being here? Oh Susie, I'm so sorry. I wasn't thinking." Elsie was just smiling.

Susie asked. "What's so damn funny, Elsie?" Susie never looked out onto the terrace because it was too cool to take the baby outside.

Elsie said happily, "Come Susie, it's time for you to go downstairs."

Susie asked her sister-in-law. "Do I look okay?"

Elsie answered proudly, "You look radiant."

As Susie went toward the stairs, Elsie followed behind her holding the baby in her arms. As she approached the den doors, Susie wondered how it was going to be for her birthday. With the racial differences on both sides of the family, Susie took a deep breath as she approached the den. She stepped into the den and suddenly saw Hilda and William saying, "Happy Birthday, Susie!"

Susie's hands flew to her mouth in astonishment. She almost started to cry when first her sister, and then her brother came to embrace her. She hugged them with so much excitement and said, "Oh, my brother and sister came to see me!" The room was fully decorated with a ten-foot tree in the middle of the room. With the wine colored walls, the boughs were decorated over the fireplace with the holly. There were berries hanging along with the stockings for everybody in the house.

Elton was not there, of course. He thought that Elijah would come to the house, so he left early. Elton tolerated Susie because of John. Knowing that she was Indian, Elton knew what kind of woman Susie was. She was an outspoken woman that he knew one day that he would have to catch doing something, so that he could gain power over her. John knew it too, but he was just waiting on that right time to see it.

Mother Quinton exclaimed, "Let's make a toast. To Susie, may she have many birthdays in this house." Everybody toasted with wine in the most beautiful rose-colored goblets that Mother Quinton put out for the occasion.

Hilda held her nephew in her arms and remarked, "Susie, he looks just like Daddy." She smiled so proudly. "Look at his ears." Hilda laughed out loud while Mother Quinton sneered.

Elsie said, "He's named after me."

Hilda looked at Susie with a measured expression of distaste. "Yes," Hilda reluctantly answered Elsie. "But I'll bet that he won't ACT like you."

Elsie looked embarrassed. William walked over to pick up and cradle his nephew.

Elton Fitzgerald Quinton was just two months old. He was a strong child. He was admiring the room without a sound coming out of his mouth. This baby liked the many-colored lights around the house. They seemed to calm him, and he serenely received the attention from his family. However, he was too preoccupied with all the people loving on him to notice that not everyone wanted his eyes on them. Mother Quinton had not held the baby since it was born. She only glared at the baby from a distance.

Hilda realized that fact, and so did William. Everybody was gathering around on Susie's birthday until the African women brought in a four-tier cake. Everybody marveled at how lovely the cake was. As the evening went on, John and William walked out on the terrace of the house to talk. William paused to look at John; they had not talked to each other in a long time. John looked at William sincerely.

"So, I guess everything is fine between the two of you?" William waited for John to answer.

"Yeah, everything is okay. I told you that I was going to take care of Susie. William, just say what's on your mind."

William replied, "John, there's something strange going on here in Tallahassee when it comes to these black folks living here. People are getting run off their land."

"Why are you telling me this?" John asked with contempt. "William, I don't know what's going on, but I'm going to get to the bottom of it."

William shook his head with disgust. "I hope that you don't think that I'm in the middle of this!" John exclaimed.

William turned to look at John. "Well, are you?" William asked him directly. "You've changed, John, since you have gotten back here. You don't contact me as you used to. What's really going on? Oh, I forgot: you're white and I'm Indian, right?" William was getting angry. "Let me tell you something. As long as my sister is with you, I'm not going to hold back, when it comes to your daddy." William walked away from John to go back into the house to join everybody.

John stood alone and looked out on the land that his father had acquired for them. Through the years that he had spent in this house, which was all of his life, he saw that it was all a façade of pure hopelessness and pain. Everybody was in the den laughing and having a good time, but John knew that Elton was in town at the parlor with another woman. John knew why his father visited there.

It was getting late. Susie showed Hilda her bedroom, and Hilda knew she was in a different place from where she came from. Hilda said to Susie, "This is beautiful! No wonder you wanted to live here, Susie." As Hilda walks out to the terrace, she saw the carriage right in front of the house.

"Hilda, I hope I see you this spring at the white folks' festival," Susie said. "I love you, and take care of Daddy, okay?" As William and Hilda left the Quinton Mansion, they waved goodbye as Susie watched her family go down the road.

John closed up the house for the night. Because Elton hadn't come home yet, Elsie stayed down in the den to wait for him. John came into the bedroom and saw Susie sitting on the side of the bed. Little Elton was sleeping silently. Susie looked up at her husband and she started to cry; her husband took her into his arms. Susie said gratefully, "Thank you for this wonderful evening, John."

John held his wife tight. He wondered what it would have been like had he, too, not come home on his wife's birthday. He decided then that he was not going to be like his father. John had watched his father neglect his mother for years, and even though he knew what his father was doing to the people in Okeechobee County, he was going to make sure that he does not do it to his family.

"Susie, I love you. I really do. You have given me a beautiful son. No matter whom he looks like, he is mine. It has been a long time since I have touched you. Susie, I need you right now." John held himself back momentarily to look at his wife; he wanted her to see that he still desired her, with his blue eyes glazing in the light of the lamp that glowed next to their bed. Susie stood, took off her dress, and looked at John hungrily.

As they got into bed, John grabbed Susie by her hair and kissed her passionately. They looked at each other with eyes that felt the ecstasy of their hearts beating for each other. As they began to make love to each other, the baby started to cry, and John got up out of the bed to tend to his son. The baby cooed when he saw his Daddy; the baby smiled at his father and grabbed him by his ears to try to pull them off. Susie admired her two men from the bed. John put the baby back to sleep and resumed making love to his wife.

It was early spring in 1922. President Wilson had been re-elected to another term. Blacks were praying to God. Wilson had his "Klan" working for him, too. Not much could be said about him except the fact that relations weren't good for the black man nor the Indians. Louis Armstrong was twelve years old. Satchel Paige, the famous black baseball player, was only six years old at the time.

Also during this time, there were two black men who were vaudeville entertainers named Bert William and George Walker. My great-grandmother Susie lived in the South, and these men were up north in New York performing. Be that as it may, the newspapers hit fast to know what was going on in the entertainment world.

There was also this black man named Marcus Garvey that was stirring up a lot attention in New York. He was the black man's "Messiah." Consequently, the southerners tried very hard to keep news from blacks about what was going on in the North. After the Civil War, white southerners began to support and enforce something called "Jim Crow Law." It was a law that kept blacks separated from the whites in economics, education and housing.

One morning Elton came to breakfast very upset. The family looked at him with disgust and shame. It was chilly outside even though it was spring. The trees swayed in the breeze, as the wind blowing was making another sound, as if it was mad about something. The slaves didn't come around unless they were called by their "massah." Somehow, some of the blacks in Okeechobee County knew what was going on, and John was hearing about a lot of things. Especially what happened to Mr. Jefferson's land; the Klan ran him man off his land. They didn't kill him. They just set all of his possessions up in flames.

As Elton read the paper, everybody was silent. Even Mother Quinton refrained from speaking. She stared at her husband eating breakfast and wiped her mouth carefully. Mother Quinton asked her husband quizzically, "Elton Quinton, what in the world is wrong with you?"

Elton put the paper down and turned to look at her with his eyes piercing through hers. Elton announced angrily, "I didn't have anything to do with Mr. Jefferson's land. Everybody is pointing their finger at me! John, I promise you, I thought everything went well with the land deal."

John had to swallow the food in his mouth in order to answer his father. John wiped his mouth. Susie was looking at her husband to hear what he had to say. "Well, Father, I was told that the lawyer – what's his name? He made Mr. Jefferson an offer, but Mr. Jefferson refused it."

Elton stood up from the table and rubbed his beard as he walked toward the window. "Ladies, would you excuse us please?" Susie, Elsie, and Mother Quinton left the room with their noses in the air in disdain, but they only went as far as the hallway so they could listen.

Elton said angrily, "Damn it, John! I have to be elected to that seat in the county courthouse, and I will be damned if you or anyone else try to stop me.

"Every time I turn around, folk are saying it's my fault for what is going on here in Okeechobee County. Now that we've gotten rid of the Indians, now its black folk. I'm not going to stand for it. You're going to help me get that seat. Tomorrow morning, I'll get in touch with McElroy and find out what the hell happened."

The women hurried into the den to talk about what they had just heard. Mother Quinton knew that her husband had his hand in it. She just didn't tell her daughter or daughter-in-law, afraid that something could happen. Susie knew that she needed to get in touch with William to let him know and to make sure that her people were okay. Susie knew something was up, but she couldn't put her finger on it right then. She thought about her baby, and if she would have more children by John.

The April festival was near. The people in Tallahassee were getting anxious. After the commotion about Mr. Jefferson, the blacks were starting to get outspoken about social issues in the town. While they lived on the west side of town, across the railroad tracks with the dirt roads, the whites were living on the east side with concrete roads, and business flowed through the town.

Susie and Elsie prepared to go to the festival. Susie was missing her family deeply. As she dressed the baby, John came in quietly and asked his wife, "Are you ready to go into town?"

Susie looked at her husband and took a deep breath. "Yes, I'm ready." Mother Quinton didn't want to go. She was in the den drinking again. As they said goodbye to her, John placed his wife in the carriage while Elsie climbed into the back and sat quietly.

Elsie started to say. "You're going to like OUR festival Susie. I hope that we won't miss the parade." She giggled and continued. Wait until you see the booths to buy something nice for yourself, Susie." Susie just looked at her son as he was cooing in his mother's arms. John was driving the horses, not saying a word.

As they approached the town, it was a very hot that day. No breeze, no wind – only steaming heat blazing onto the ground. People were walking toward town. The women with their parasols and matching dresses were looking elegant on the hot spring day; they wore their bonnets to keep the sun out of their face. John got to the place to park his carriage; the black man came to John and John gave him one dollar to tend to his horse and buggy.

They all walked to the front of the courthouse where they could to sit on the bleachers to see the parade. The town was decorated with all kinds of flowers outside of the storefronts. Balloons were everywhere, and the baby was silently in awe looking at them. The parade has started while the town band played that old Civil War song called "Dixieland." Susie was about to get sick until she held her breath, and she looked down at little Elton in her arms. Elsie noticed that Susie didn't like that song.

As the clowns and horses started to come up the street, John told Susie that he would be back.

Susie smiled, agreeing with him, and looked up to see that some Indians were coming up the street. She rose up from her seat to see whom she could see. Elsie watched Susie cheer for her people. People started to look at Susie as if she was doing something embarrassing. Susie didn't care because she was proud of her people. Yes! She saw some of Running Bear's grandchildren and a few others. Susie was waving her handkerchief at them.

The parade was over and everybody was getting up to leave to go up and down the street for more festivities. All of a sudden Susie asks, "Where's John?" Elsie tried to answer but she didn't know. Instead, Elsie replied, "Let me show you this booth that has crystal glass everything."

Susie followed Elsie to see what the booth had. It had a beautiful vase with a magnolia flower that was stained white.

Susie said excitedly, "Elsie, it's beautiful."

"You want it?" Elsie took out her money to purchase the item.

Susie said, "Thank you, Elsie."

Elsie said, "I'll be back. Don't go far." Susie looked around to see what else that she could see. She was noticing all kinds of booths that she could visit. She turned around to see someone at an Indian booth. As she walks over slowly, she saw that it was Little Feather. Susie gasped under her breath as she walked towards the booth. Little Feather did not see her at first. As she neared the booth, she held the baby close to her.

Little Feather was waiting on some young children. When he saw her, he stopped paying attention to what he was doing. He finished serving the kids and sent them on their way. Susie arrived at the booth. Little Feather's heart beat rapidly. He stared intensely at Susie with his deep hazel eyes, and Susie was looking at Little Feather the same way.

"Hello, Susie. I was hoping that I would see you today. You look so beautiful. I miss you deeply. Is there any way that I could see you and talk? Your daddy is getting old and cranky."

Susie replied tiredly, "I know. I feel him in my heart. Have you seen William?"

Little Feather shook his head no. He picked up a beautiful turquoise necklace and put it around Susie's neck.

"I want you to wear this forever for me." Little Feather looked at Susie while he puts the necklace on her. "Susie, I can't take this any longer. Are you sure this baby isn't mine? He looks just like us."

"Little Feather, don't say that because this isn't the time or place for such talk." Susie looked at Little Feather longingly. She said, "Look, I must get back because it's too hot outside for the baby. I will see you again - trust me." As she turned around leave, she stopped to tell Little

Feather, "Thank you for the necklace." Susie puts the necklace under her collar of her dress so that John wouldn't see it.

Little Feather watched Susie leave and did not take his eyes off her until she was out of sight. Elsie finally approached. "Sister, I've been looking for you."

"Where's John?" Susie asked impatiently.

"I don't know."

"I'm ready to leave now."

Elsie said excitedly, "Oh no, Susie! We have to stay and see the fireworks!"

Susie answered back, "I've seen enough fireworks for the day." Susie was thinking about Little Feather.

Chapter 15

John Confronts a Black Woman

As they neared the courthouse, Susie saw John in what looked like an animated conversation with a dark-skinned woman. The woman appeared very angry. Susie didn't point them out to Elsie, but she discreetly watched them together. The woman snatched her arm from John and walked away. John looked frustrated and he took a deep breath and look around, but didn't see Elsie and his wife. Susie deliberately made her way towards John, for there were a lot of people in the street.

John finally saw Susie and Elsie. The baby was crying by this time because it was very hot outside. Susie stared at John, because John had left them an hour before. John came up to see his son getting flustered with the heat. "I've been looking for you two."

Susie just stared at John. "I'm ready to leave, John."

John was taken aback. "No, honey, let's stay and watch the fireworks."

Elsie said, "That's what I told her."

"The baby's tired and I am too." Susie walked away from both of them. Elsie knew then that Susie had seen John with that dark-skinned woman.

As they climbed into the carriage, the baby was crying loudly. The horses were pulling the carriage at a gallop; a little breeze moved through the buggy and helped the baby to drift off to sleep. Susie stared at her husband. Elsie watched the both of them and attempted to break the cold silence during their ride home. "Well, Susie how did you like our festival?"

Susie was just staring at John while John was feeling the heat from his wife's emotions.

"Elsie, I'm sorry. I am preoccupied at this moment," Susie replied. "It was okay. It would've been better had my husband not disappeared." John frowned at Susie frowning but kept the carriage moving. Elsie looked at John because she knew about him with this mysterious black woman.

Elsie interjected, "Whew! I'm glad that we're almost home."

The baby was fast asleep on this hot day. The clouds were gray and heavy, signaling rain. As the sun went behind the clouds, the trees started to sway back and forth. John pulled up the road about fifty feet from the house. Susie looked at her husband again with such an intense look that Elsie could not wait to get out of the carriage to tell Mother Quinton what went on.

They approached the house and the helpers came out to greet them. Mother Quinton was sitting on the beautiful porch and she stood up;

Elsie's face told her something had happened. Elsie went into the house. Susie was getting help from one of the black maids with the baby. Susie greeted Mother Quinton and went into the house to tend to the baby.

Mother Quinton asked John, "What in the world happened?" The winds were fierce as they went into the house quickly.

John took his mother into the den and closed the doors. John rushed up to his mother and took her by the arm. "Mother, I can't take this anymore. I think Susie saw me with Patty."

Mother Quinton raised her hand to her mouth. She went to get her a drink. As she pours the drink hurriedly, the rain was coming down. The thunder was getting louder and the lights were blinking on and off.

"John, go see if everything is alright," his mother instructed him. "Get the help to light some candles. Come back and I'll talk to you."

John ran upstairs to see about his family. Susie was so angry and hurt by what she had seen of John. The lightning struck in the bedroom as Susie grabbed the baby and held him tightly. Her voice was tight as she looked up at him and growled, "I would love to hear what you've got to say."

The rain was coming down heavily. John looked at his wife, trying to think what he was going to say.

"Susie, it's not what you think," John said.

Susie snatched away from John's arms. "Oh yeah! Well, John when they say like father like son, it surely does stand true in this family! I am not going to stand for it. You tell me what's going on right now!"

John could not meet his Susie's eyes. He turned away momentarily from his wife, saying, "Susie, I can't. You've just got to trust me." He turned back and walked toward her, but it was

231

Susie's time to turn away. John left her to go see his Mother again.

Elsie was listening as she watched John go down the stairs. Elsie went into their bedroom and saw Susie crying. Elsie went to her sister-in-law held her while Susie cried. Elsie said to Susie, "I'm quite sure that there is a good explanation for this."

Susie stopped crying for a moment. "You did see her. Do you know her?"

Elsie answered, "No, I don't. Susie, please do not leave. You know you could have another baby, and maybe he'll stop seeing her."

Susie shed tears now of frustration. "Elsie, that's old thinking. A man is going to do what they want to do anyway. No matter what you do as a wife." She looked pointedly at her sister-in-law. "Where's your Daddy?"

Elsie looked puzzled at Susie, "I don't know. I really have no idea."

Susie replied, "That's my point." She shook her head at Elsie dismissively. "I'll be alright. Really." The rain had stopped. Susie walked out onto the terrace to shut the doors so that the breeze would not wake up the baby. Elsie left the bedroom to go downstairs to the den.

By this time, Mother Quinton was on her third drink as she was talking to John. She turned around to her son. "John, you got to be more careful. Jenny has been staying with her all this time and you have fallen in love with her. If the people find out that you are having an affair with this woman it would be the death of you and this family."

As Elsie came to the den doors, she heard what her mother had said. Elsie's eyes got big as she held her mouth with her hand. She stayed in the corridor to hear the rest of it. John turned around, brushing his hair to the back of his head with one hand. "Mother, I'll do my best. Because I love my wife; I don't want to hurt her."

Mother Quinton answered, "Too late, son. You've already done that."

Elton was coming in the door. Elsie hurried and ran into the kitchen as if she was looking for something to eat. Elton comes in. "Everything all right?"

Elsie looked at her Daddy and rolled her eyes toward the ceiling. The question exasperated her. "Why do you care? You're never here to find out."

Elton was taken aback by Elsie's words. "Don't get smart with me, missy." He looked around. "Where's John and your mother?"

Elsie drank her tea and swallowed, "They're in the den."

Elton went into the den to find his wife and son in very intense conversation. He looked at his wife and saw that she had been drinking. "What's going on?"

Mother Quinton walked drunkenly over to her husband. "Darling, you've come home. Well, I'm shocked to see that you care about your family."

Elton turned to his son. "John, what's going on?"

John answers his father with a sad voice. "Dad, I think Susie saw me with Patty today at the festival."

Elton laughs so hard that he starts coughing. "Is that all? Well, hell, I thought you was leaving her."

Mother Quinton hollered. "Elton! This isn't funny!"

Elton walked over to his son. "Whatever you do John, don't tell Susie nothing. I will talk to her in the morning. Right now, I am going to bed. Darling, aren't you coming?" Mother Quinton put her glass down on the table. Mother Quinton embraced her son and followed her husband out of the den.

The morning was very cool. John slept on the sofa in their bedroom; Susie awoke and saw her husband still sleeping. She was shocked to see that he hadn't left early that morning as had become his custom. The baby woke up and the black maids came in to serve them breakfast. John was snoring. Susie walked over to her husband and tapped him on the side of his head. John jumped up quickly.

"Good morning, Mr. John." The black maid said happily.

"Good morning!" John looked at Susie painfully. Susie ignored her husband as the maids helped her to get dressed. Susie put on this yellow-laced dress with white fringe on her sleeves. She fixed her hair into a Victorian bun with white beads in it. Susie went to the baby to get him dressed. John asked confusedly, "Where are you going?"

Susie did not answer his question as the maids left the room. "Do I ask you where you're going, John?

When the carriage was ready for Susie, she grabbed the baby, walked out of the bedroom and slammed the door. Elton was meeting her at the bottom of the stairs, and his greeting was filled with sarcasm. "My headstrong, willful daughter-in-law, may I ask where you're going?"

Susie pointedly replied, "No, you may not." Without a smile or a grin, Susie walked past her father-in-law to the front door.

The black driver helped her into the carriage and then drove off swiftly. Susie was going to town to find out who this woman was. She had to find out. She was going to see William too because she had not seen him in months. Her father was getting old and tired. Susie finally realized what she had gotten herself involved in. She could have stayed on her Daddy's "porch" where it was peaceful and serene, and the older Indian women would come and be free and happy, even when times were hard. It sure was not like the "porch" that the Quintons had, with the chaos, confusion, racial tension, and deceit.

As she entered the town plaza, women were on the street whispering, but Susie did not care. She was going to find out whom this mysterious woman was. She directed the black driver to William's office; William saw her coming. He rushed out to greet her. "Susie! What are you doing here so early in the morning?" He opened the door to let her in. At the sight of her brother, she burst into tears.

"William, it's so good to see you! Where have you been doing?"

"Susie, I've been awfully busy. The blacks are coming to me for help in their affairs. It's been crazy here lately."

"Tell me about it," she said as she sat the baby down in John's big leather chair. "William, John's having an affair. I'm here for you to help me find out who she is."

William looked astonished. "What do you mean John is having an affair? Just because you saw him with another woman doesn't mean he's having an affair."

Susie sighed. "I'm not ignorant William. Whoever she is, something tells me that it's got something to do with Jenny. Remember Jenny?"

William walked over to take his nephew from Susie. The baby gurgled and cooed for his

Uncle. William asked his sister, "What do you want me to do?"

"I want you to find out who she is William!"

William rubbed his hand over his face. "Okay, I'll do the best that I can. You need to get back to your home before your husband's family gets worried."

"I don't give a damn about what they think," his sister retorted. "I'm getting sick of them." Susie walked over to get the baby when, outside the window, she sees the mysterious woman. Susie exclaims, "There she is, William!" Before William could go after Susie, Susie rushed out the door and ran across the street. William stopped because little Elton was in the chair laughing at his Uncle.

Susie walked quickly to catch up with the woman. The woman was going into the Parlor. Susie ran up to her. "Excuse me, Excuse me!"

The woman turned around to Susie; the woman's eyes were a dark hazel brown. The woman furrowed her brows at Susie. "What do you want?"

Susie looked at the woman to let her know that she wasn't scared of her. "I want to know who you are!"

The woman looked at Susie up and down. "Why do you want to know?"

Susie took a deep breath. "I saw you with my husband at the festival and I want to know who you are."

"Ahhh," said the woman. She started to smile. When she smiled, she looked even more mysterious. "Why do you want to know?"

Susie replied, "Look, I don't play games with anyone. When I see a mysterious woman like you with my husband, I think I have a right to know what's going on."

The woman still smiled, knowingly, but her expression gave away nothing else. "You need to ask your husband. If you will excuse me." The woman turned away from Susie and went into the Parlor.

Susie looked flustered. "I know what you look like. Remember that!" The woman ignored Susie, and the door closed behind her in Susie's face. Susie picked up her dress to hold it and walked across the street to get her baby. William was still holding the baby; Susie took little Elton from her brother's arms, but her gaze was drawn back toward the street. William just chuckled and shook his head. William said, "I think I know who she is. If you didn't rush out of here, I would've told you who she was."

Susie turned around quickly. "Who is she?"

"A long time ago, I mean a long time ago, when John and I were kids, I saw that woman and Eleanor together." William walked around his desk and continued. "That woman, I believe, is taking care of Jenny."

Susie's face was a mixture of shock and triumph. "I knew it! Boy, you talk about having wit."

William walked over to Susie and put his hand on her shoulder, "Susie, you must not go any further with this. I vowed to John that I would not tell you. Please Susie, do not pressure him about this. I'm quite sure that it will come to light someday."

Susie exclaimed. "Oh, I'm quite sure it will! The more I stay in this crazy family, the better it gets. But I promise that I won't say anything."

William said, "Good girl. Now go home, will ya?" He kissed his sister on the cheek.

Susie arrived home to find a quiet house. Mother Quinton was in the backyard, on the swing in the gazebo. Elsie was with her, talking. Susie walked out toward the gazebo, and Elsie stopped talking. Susie said, "Don't stop talking because of me." Elsie smiled. She takes her nephew out of Susie's arms.

Mother Quinton looked at Susie. "Sit down dear, let me tell you something." Susie took a seat next to her mother-in-law.

"When a woman has a baby, she gets very vulnerable. I thought I was so strong being with Elton. Over the years, times get so hard that you are just stuck with your feelings. Men do not know how to deal with our emotions. I know that I did not like you at first, Susie, but I see that you are different and that is not just, because you are an Indian. It's your spirit that doesn't stop you from doing what you want to do."

Eleanor Quinton got up from the swing. "I gave up a long time ago. Especially when Jenny had to leave here. My heart went out for her. Because she did not let love stop her, either, from getting what she wanted - and it cost her her life.

Don't let what you saw stop you from loving your man because if you do – it will cost you yours."

Chapter 16
The Roaring Twenties

Time was moving on. It was heading into the "Roaring 1920's". Susie gave birth to three daughters that she named Margaret, Geneva and baby girl Louise. They were some pretty little girls. Geneva looked exactly like her grandfather Elijah with the dark red skin and the beautiful black hair that looked blue in the sun. Margaret was white like her grandmother Mother Quinton with a protruding mouth. Little Louise a lot like her sister Margaret. Geneva was born five years after the great ship *The Titanic* sank into the Atlantic Ocean.

Baby Louise always got her way. Her two older sisters envied her, but they did not pay any attention to her because she acted like Elsie, very naïve and very reclusive. Her father loved her because she looked like Jenny. Mother Quinton and Susie were not getting along lately because of all of the children in her house. She was afraid that they would damage her house. Mother Quinton in her old age, would look at my grandmother Geneva with hatred in her eyes because she was darker than her other sisters.

Susie and John would frequently argue because Susie wanted John to get them their own house; she felt that it was time. John finally agreed, and they selected a plot of land between his parent's mansion and the town. That suited Susie better. Even Elsie was getting frustrated, but she loved her nieces and nephew. Little Elton was growing to be quite a good-looking young man. He looked just like the Quintons from head to toe, in spite of those large Indian ears. Elton would study hard in school because he knew what he was going to do. His plan was to get away from his family as soon as possible.

While the house was being built, Susie was packing her belongings, ready to go. Elsie came in the bedroom looking sad. "I'm sorry that you're leaving Susie. I hope that I can come to visit you and the children." Elsie walked around the bedroom reminiscing about the times that they spent in the bedroom talking while Susie continued to pack.

Susie started feeling a little melancholy about what Elsie was talking about and Elsie continued, "You remember when you first came here and how you felt so happy. I hope that you feel that same feeling about John."

Susie stopped to look at Elsie, and said, "Elsie, times have changed. Your daddy is getting ready to lose his seat in government, and the rest of this God-forsaken family is going down. I've got to look out for my children now. I don't care what the town thinks of me or anything else. I've been working for my people, watching and listening to the upper-class white women whisper behind my back, running their mouths about social issues – all of it has made me sick." She took a breath and said, "Of course, you can come to see us. I'll be glad when you do. Elsie, do you know what's going on in the outside world beside our own?"

Without waiting for her sister-in-law to answer, Susie continued, "Well, I've heard there's this black man named Marcus Garvey in New York telling black folks that they need to go back to Africa. They have been rioting up there! Then these women named Susan B. Anthony, Ida B. Wells and Mary McLeod Bethune have been marching in New York fighting for the Women's Suffrage so that we can vote. Did you know about any of that?" Susie asked her sister-in-law.

Elsie looked shocked that Susie has been reading a lot. Elsie answered with a puzzled expression. "Yes Susie, but what that got to do with us? Yes, I know that black folks are tired of what's going on with them. I personally thought that they liked working for us."

Susie turned to look at her. "Elsie, you don't get it do you? Your mama and daddy have messed your mind up so bad, you don't know whether you're coming or going."

Susie started to get angry as she thought of how Elsie was raised, "Pretty soon, things are going to get ugly around here. Can't you see how they treat black folks down here? I don't need to start talking about how they've treated MY people for years. I don't mean to be angry, Elsie, but it's time for me to get out of here."

When the house was ready, Susie took her children out of that mansion and never looked back. Elsie started to cry and Mother Quinton had a smirk on her face. Susie approached the new house that John had built for them. It was a cottage with a long porch, where John had made a swing for Susie. As they were moving in, Elsie came over to help. Susie lived near some black folks that just watched from a distance. They knew to whom she was married. They thought that Susie was a snob, just like the other white folks.

As Susie got settled in, one of her neighbors she met was this black man named Mr. Bill. Mr. Bill had five children and a wife. He made his living working on white people's lawns. Mr. Bill came walking over toward the porch. Susie noticed that he was a tall, dark man with an old brim on his head. "Hi, my name is Mr. Bill. I lived across the street and I came over to say welcome to the neighborhood."

Susie didn't shake his hand. In fact, she'd never shook a black man's hand before in her life. She spoke kindly. "I'm much obliged to meet you. What do you do around here?"

Mr. Bill took off his hat and waited to see if Susie would invite him onto the porch, but she didn't. Mr. Bill answers politely. "Well ma'am, I do lawns. Any and everything that you want me to do."

Susie looked at Mr. Bill with her hands on her slim hips. "Well, I do have some things that I need you to do. Can you move furniture?"

The cottage house was white with a long porch that only had two columns. The roof of the porch stood out with a big window in the front from the upstairs. Susie had a little foyer coming inside her living room with a fireplace that was made out of stone instead of bricks. The children were pleased with their bedrooms. The kitchen was a nice size. As long you can put a table and five chairs in there, it was big enough. Mr. Bill did a good job helping Susie. By John being gone all the time, Susie had to do what she had to do to get her house in order.

The Roaring Twenties were roaring. Susie played music from artist of the time: Bessie Smith,

Charlie Parker, and Ethel Waters on her Victrola. Louis "Satchmo Armstrong was hitting big in Chicago. There was an artist whom people referred to as "Sir Duke." Duke Ellington was his name and he had an orchestra in New York. It was the time of the Harlem Renaissance. Blacks were expressing themselves through art, literature and music. There were a number of black writers such as Zora Neale Hurston, Langston Hughes, Wallace Thurman, James Baldwin and Countee Cullen. All wrote powerful literature about black life and culture in a world where many people grasped to hold on to what they had during those days of Jim Crow. The Italians were taking over New York and Chicago trying to gain respect through the underworld of crime and extortion.

There was a black woman name Bessie Coleman who, in 1921, became the first black female pilot. There was a black man that worked with Thomas Edison to engineer the electric light bulb. The Roaring 20's brought such devastating and remarkable times for blacks, Italians, and for the white man.

Susie was educating Mr. Bill about these innovative people in their time. Learning about what other people were doing in the world began to give Mr. Bill a sense of pride in himself. His family and Susie and her children related well together. John noticed that Elsie spent more time at their house than she did at her own family's home. In spite of everything, everybody worked to get along and stay together. Through the good times and the bad times, the people in Tallahassee started to give Miss Susie the respect that she earned by being an Indian in the white man's world.

When everybody was leaving, Susie and Elsie started to clean up. As they put the children to bed, Susie started thinking about what John could be. She thought about how Elton treated Mother Quinton, and she knew that she wouldn't allow John to treat her like that. She had made plans to go out this evening. Susie asked Elsie stay overnight and watch the kids. Elsie gladly said, "Yes! I thought you'd never ask."

"Wonderful! I won't be long," Susie said.

When Elsie went upstairs to go to bed, Susie went into the closet to get some of John's clothes to put on. As she struck out down the road, some men were coming her way. She turned her head and pulled her hat down on her face; she wanted no one to know that she was a woman. When she arrived in town, a lot of white men were standing in front of the town's square talking and nodding their heads.

Susie stood back to watch and see what was going on. Apparently, a black man was to have stolen some of Mr. Johnson's chickens. Be as it may, the man had a family that were starving. As Susie continued to listen, she sees John. She turned her head and moved over to behind a pole in front of the hardware store.

There were no women in the town square except the women at the Parlor watching from the front door. Susie kept her eye on the "Parlor" to see if she sees Patty. Susie stood there until a wagon came holding black man on the back tied up like some animal. "Kill him! Kill him!" The crowd was loud with sticks in the hand with fire burning at the end of them.

Some men came toward the wagon dressed in white with hoods over their heads. Susie was so shocked that she almost forgot that she was a woman dressed in men's clothing.

All of a sudden, she heard a familiar voice. "Everybody listen up! This nigger was caught stealing Mr. Johnson's chickens. What shall we do about it?"

"Hang him! Hang him!" The chanting crowd was out of control as they took the black man and hung him right in front of town's square.

Susie tried to get out of the way when she bumped into a white man. As Susie left, the man remarked, "That's a strange man to have some perfume on like a lady." The man watched Susie run down the street. Susie was gasping for air and crying at the same time. She was holding her hand to her mouth trying not to scream at what she saw.

When she approached the house, she snuck in quietly and hurried to get out of her husband's clothes. She quickly dressed in her gown before Elsie heard Susie in the house. Elsie came downstairs sleepily. "You're back?"

Susie still looking still frightened, not knowing what to say. Elsie felt something was wrong. "Are you all right Susie?" Elsie looked closely at her sister-in-law. "Don't tell me that you went into town."

Susie was so upset that her heart was beating like a fast freight train. "So what if I did Elsie? Your daddy is going to pay for a lot of things. You watch what I'm telling you." Susie was pacing around the kitchen table.

`Elsie said contritely, "Susie, I'm so sorry."

Susie replied, "If I had have known, I wouldn't married John for this! Now, things are coming to the light, and I'm going to see to it that I'm not going to back down from YOUR father."

The KKK

The morning came fast with the trees bending in a breeze blowing so soft and smooth. Susie sat on her porch just thinking about the night before. Elsie left early in the morning. Susie didn't care because she knew that it was all over. She had fed her children and was letting them play in the yard when all of a sudden, ten white men was rode up to the house on their horses. The people in the neighborhood ran into their homes. Susie stayed outside.

The posse stopped right in front of her house with hatred in their eyes. My great-grandmother Susie stood up and told her children not to move. The white men knew who she was. They hated Susie's rebellious strength in standing up to them. She put her hands on her hips to ask them, "Do you have a problem?" The children stood behind her, frightened. Elton started to say something. Susie said to him, "Don't say a word." The white men turned their horses and rode away as they left dust on the road.

Susie's neighbors came back outside and saw what Susie had done. They knew who she was married to, but they couldn't understand why those men treated her like that. Susie knew for certain, at that encounter, that Elton was a Klansman. Mr. Bill ran over to Susie's house. "Miss Susie, are you all right?"

"Yeah Bill, I'm fine. You know what? My daddy and that Elton Quinton hate each other to this day. My daddy told me not to kiss nobody's ass. He is full-bred Cherokee and I'm not going to ever forget that. When I was up there in the Mansion watching those black women serving the family, I would hear them talking about my people and yours. When John gets home, we're going to have a talk because if they do anything to me and mine, I will see to it that the Quinton Mansion is destroyed!" Susie exclaimed.

Bill, with his eyes bulging out, swallowed hard and said, "Miss Susie, you don't mean that."

William came riding up on his horse. Mr. Bill went to greet William and William tipped his hat to Mr. Bill. He dismounted his horse and said, "Susie, I need to talk to you right now!"

Mr. Bill got up from Susie's porch, where he was sitting, to leave. At his departure, Susie took William into the living room. "Susie, brace yourself. Daddy is dying, and he wants to see you."

It was as if a cold, iron fist grabbed Susie around her heart at the news. "Oh, my God!" She swiftly gathered up the children and went with her brother to the Indian village.

The children were excited, for they never have been to the home where their mother grew up. Elton had visited, but it didn't bother him any, because he felt that he was white, and not an Indian. Margaret looked white, so it didn't make her any difference to her either, but it was Geneva that looked like her people with her dark, red skin and her hair that turned blue in the sun. She didn't know any difference because she was too little to realize it. Elsie had come to get little Louise to take her to the mansion.

Chapter 17
Elijah Dies

As they arrived at the village, the old Indians were living in their rundown shacks for homes; the young Indians had left the village, so no one was there to care for the properties. The absence of youth left the place desolate and without life. The flowers on Elijah's porch were dead. Hilda wasn't taking care of them like she used to. While the other children waited and sat on the porch, little Elton went right on inside the house. He noticed that the house had a peculiar smell. He came right back out to play around the house as he looked out at the hills and valleys. Elton sat on the ground with a tear in his eye.

Susie approached the dark room as her father lay dying. Hilda went over to the left side of Elijah's bed. Elijah awoke and started to speak with a hoarse voice. "My girls, the time has come for me to join my Snow Feather." Tears were coming down his daughters' faces. "I want you girls to burn this house after you all take what y'all want. All that I have belongs you both; take what you want and get away from here. I've seen a vision that Tallahassee is going to be in trouble and I don't want y'all to be a part of it. Go to Louisville, Kentucky, where your brothers are. I love you both, forever." Then Elijah, the Great One, took his last breath.

The funeral was a sad one. Little Feather came. Running Bear, who could hardly see or walk, was present. There were some old Indians in attendance who just stared at Susie. They resented her for leaving her father and marrying a white man. They paid their respects, and then left without saying a word. Susie knew why they looked at her the way they did. Still, she sat proudly in front of her fathers' casket. She was filled with regret, and the tears kept rolling down her cheeks. She wiped them away.

William, Hilda, and Susie gathered everything they could so that they could carry out their father's wishes. As the house was burning, the people gathered around to chant in Indian language about their beloved Elijah and for him to go to the "Great Spirit." When everything was said and done, the children of Elijah Poohtawn quietly left the village. Little Feather didn't speak to Susie this time. He just left like an Indian. After walking into the woods, Little Feather looked up in the sky and saw a star fall from the sky. Little Feather left without saying goodbye.

The Indians all saw the falling star as they walked to their homes in the settlement quietly. It is said that when you see a falling star, someone great or famous has died. Elijah was a great leader to his people. Like Moses in the Bible, Elijah made sure that his people were going to be taken care of. Hilda stayed with William until they decided on the date they were going to leave Tallahassee. She didn't want to stay with Susie, because Susie had too many children to deal with. She didn't tell her sister or brother that she was pregnant.

As William returned Susie home, John was waiting for her and the children were waiting patiently. While they watched their mother come up to the porch, they ran out to greet her. She hugged her children and just cried in their arms. John took her inside the house to lie down. William sat on the porch and bowed his head. John came back out on the porch. "I'm sorry, Will, about your father."

William tells John, "A star fell out of the sky. Do you know what that means John?" John nodded his head to say yes.

John said, "Your father was a Great Warrior."

William said, "I heard what happened in town and this morning, John. My daddy may be dead and gone, but if Elton does anything to my sister, I'll swear to you he'll regret it."

John said, "I can't do anything with Susie. I told Daddy that!"

William got up chuckling. "I know." He put his hat on his head and got onto his horse to leave.

Three months later, Mother Quinton died. They had her body at the mansion and buried her near her parents in the white graveyard. John took Elsie out to the gazebo. She was in a daze, not saying anything. All she could do is shake her head in despair. She wondered then what would to happen to her. She knew that Susie would be leaving soon. Elsie had tried to care for her father, but she couldn't. She was aware of what he had done down through the years, and since that the black maids had left, the house had turned so empty and cold. The beautiful porch was now dead.

John bowed his head and walked over to Elsie to take her hands to hold them in his. "Elsie, you know Daddy is going to sell the mansion." Elsie remained silent. John sighed. "Elsie, I know where Jenny is." Elsie looked up at her brother. "That woman Patty is taking care of her." Elsie's eyes, at hearing this news, first widened then narrowed at John. She snatched her hands away from him and got up. "How could you keep this from me? You know how much I've wanted to know!"

John stepped in front of his sister. "Elsie, if I had told you, Daddy would've taken both me and you out of his will! I did this for us Elsie!" Elsie slapped her brother across his face. As she collapsed down onto the gazebo floor, John got down on the floor with her and held her as she sobbed on his shoulder.

Elsie stopped crying long enough to say, "I'm going to go get her. I can't take this anymore!" She broke away from her brother and ran up to the mansion to see Elton.

"Don't Elsie!" screamed John.

John ran after her his sister. Elsie burst into the den and found her father drinking. Elsie slapped the drink out of his hand. "You wretched old man. After you sell this monstrosity of a home, I hope you rot in hell."

Elton couldn't say anything. He looked at John, and broke down and cried. His father looked so pitiful, that John walked over to his father to put his hand on his shoulder. Elsie went upstairs to pack her things to leave the mansion.

The next morning, people came from miles and miles around to see what they could buy from the infamous Quinton Mansion. In fact, Elton was helping them buy all of Mother Quinton's crystal, china, vases, statues, and the like. Elsie made sure that she got what she wanted. She took her Mother's jewelry and gave some of it to Hilda and Susie. She also took the bed linens and all the draperies.

People were fighting over the possessions. Susie didn't go to the mansion for the sale, because she was sure she knew what she was going to get. Instead, Susie cooked a big dinner. As she was laughing playing her blues on her Victrola, Susie invited Mr. Bill over so he could listen to the fight on the radio that a black man name Jack Johnson was fighting. Mr. Bill sat in the living room, cheering animatedly with his fists. The children were having a good time outside playing. Hilda came by to keep Susie company.

Hilda said, smiling, "Well, sister, it's almost about that time, isn't it?"

Susie stood whipping the mashed potatoes. The fried chicken smelled good. "For what?" asked Susie.

Hilda's eyes got big. "For us to leave this damned place."

Susie smiled. "Yeah, but there's some things that I have to take care of. Elsie is coming over here to give me some of Mother Quinton's bed linens and some other things. Bless that woman's heart, we didn't always get along, but I'm glad that she's gone for her own sake."

"I know what you mean," said Hilda. "I never did like her."

"Sometimes white folks can't help the way they are. They were born like that. That is why I am glad that I am an Indian. We keep our sanity while they lose theirs," Susie said, as she laughs.

"You sure are in a good mood."

Susie replied, "I have the right to be. It won't be long for Elton Fitzgerald gets his day!"

Hilda asked, quizzically, "What's that supposed to mean?"

"That's all right. You'll know in due time."
Susie just kept on laughing. Sometime later, John
and Elsie arrived, and Mr. Bill was still listening to
the fight on the radio. John went in to join Mr. Bill
by the radio.

The company of her family and the aromas
from the kitchen began to lift Elsie's spirits.
"Well, hello, my good people. Ooh! Susie, the
food smells so good! The stuff is outside. John
and Mr. Bill will bring it all inside shortly."

Susie gave Elsie a hug. "Thank you so
much." Susie kissed her on the cheek. "Dinner
will be ready in a minute."

Hilda said to Elsie, "Thank you, Elsie, for
thinking about me."

Elsie replied. "Oh, Hilda honey, we're
family, aren't we?"

The evening went well. After everybody
ate, they came out to sit on Susie's porch. John

and Bill made Susie some banisters all around the porch. She had her flowers hanging from the ceiling. Hilda went to sit down in the swing and Elsie sat in a wicker chair. Susie sat beside her sister. John and Bill were talking about the fight. Suddenly, a loud "boom" came from in the direction of the Quinton Mansion.